The
Provincial Lady
in AMERICA

★ ★
★

I say Thank you, Thank you very much, and continue to sign my name (p. 90)

THE
PROVINCIAL LADY
IN AMERICA

BY
E. M. DELAFIELD

WITH ILLUSTRATIONS
BY
MARGARET FREEMAN

Academy
Chicago
Publishers

Published in 1984 by
Academy Chicago, Publishers
425 N. Michigan Ave.
Chicago, IL 60611

Printed and bound in the USA

Library of Congress Cataloging in Publication Data

Delafield, E. M. 1890–1943.
    The provincial lady in America.

    Reprint. Originally published: New York: Harper, 1934.

    I.   Freeman, Margaret, 1893–1942.   II.   Title.
PR6007.E33P68   1984   823'.912   84-14559
ISBN 0-89733-110-9 (pbk.)

Parts of this book have already appeared in the pages of "Punch," and my thanks are due to the Editor and to the Proprietors for permission to republish.

ILLUSTRATIONS

[vii]

Illustrations

The Provincial Lady in America

The
Provincial Lady
in AMERICA

July 7th.—Incredulous astonishment on receiving by second post—usually wholly confined
to local bills and circulars concerning neighboring Garden Fêtes—courteous and charming letter from publishers in America. They
are glad to say that they feel able to meet me
on every point concerning my forthcoming visit
to the United States, and enclose contract for
my approval and signature.

Am completely thrown on my beam-ends by
this, but remember that visit to America *was*
once mooted and that I light-heartedly reeled
off stipulations as to financial requirements,
substantial advances, and so on, with no faint-
est expectation that anybody would ever pay
the slightest attention to me. This now revealed
as complete fallacy. Read contract about fourteen times running, and eyes—figuratively

[1]

speaking—nearly drop out of my head with astonishment. Can I possibly be worth all this?

Probably not, but should like to see America, and in any case am apparently committed to going there whether I want to or not.

Long and involved train of thought follows, beginning with necessity for breaking this news to Robert at the most auspicious moment possible, and going on to requirements of wardrobe, now at lowest possible ebb, and speculating as to whether, if I leave immediately after children's summer holidays, and return just before Christmas ones, it would not be advisable to embark upon Christmas shopping instantly.

All is interrupted by telephone ring—just as well, as I am rapidly becoming agitated—and voice says that it is Sorry to Disturb Me but is just Testing the Bell. I say Oh all right, and decide to show publishers' letter to Robert after tea.

Am absent-minded all through tea as a result, and give Robert sugar, which he doesn't take. He says Am I asleep or what, and I decide to postpone announcement until evening.

It rains, and presently Florence appears and

says If I please, the water's coming in on the landing through the ceiling and I say she had better go at once and find Robert—it occurs to me too late that this attitude is far from consistent with feminist views so often proclaimed by myself—and meanwhile put small basin, really Vicky's sponge-bowl, on stairs to catch water, which drips in steadily.

Return to writing-table and decide to make list of clothes required for American trip, but find myself instead making list of all the things I shall have to do before starting, beginning with passport requirements and ending with ordering China tea from the Stores, 7 lbs. cheaper than smaller quantity.

Just as I am bringing this exercise to a close Robert comes in, and shortly afterwards I hear him stumble over sponge-bowl on stairs, about which nobody has warned him. This definitely precludes breaking American news to him for the present.

He spends the evening up a ladder, looking at gutters, and I write to American publishers but decide not to post letter for a day or two.

[3]

July 8th.—Robert still unaware of impending announcement.

July 10th.—Telegram—reply pre-paid—arrives from American publishers' representative in London, enquiring what I have decided, and this is unfortunately taken down over the telephone by Robert. Full explanations ensue, are not wholly satisfactory, and am left with extraordinary sensations of guilt and duplicity which I do not attempt to analyse.

Woman called Mrs. Tressider, whom I once met and disliked when staying with Rose, writes that she will be motoring in this direction with The Boy and will call in on us about tea-time to-morrow.

(*Query:* Why not go out? *Answer:* (a) The laws of civilisation forbid (b) Such a course might lead to trouble with dear Rose (c) Cannot think of anywhere to go.)

Write, on the contrary, amiable letter to Mrs. T. saying that I look forward to seeing her and The Boy. Try to remember if I know anything whatever about the latter, but nothing materialises, not even approximate age. *Mem:* Order extra milk for tea in case he turns

[4]

out to be very young—but this not probable, from what I remember of Mrs. T.'s appearance.

Go with Robert in the afternoon to neighboring Agricultural Show, and see a good many iron implements, also a bath standing all by itself outside a tent and looking odd, and a number of animals, mostly very large. Meet the Frobishers, who say There were more people here last year, to which I agree—remember too late that I didn't come at all last year. Subsequently meet the Palmers, who say Not so many people as there were last year, and I again agree. Am slightly appalled on reflection, and wonder what would happen in the event of Frobishers and Palmers comparing notes as to their respective conversations with me—but this is unlikely in the extreme. (*Query:* Are the promptings of conscience regulated in proportion to the chances of discovery in wrong doing? *Answer:* Obviously of a cynical nature.)

We continue to look at machinery, and Robert becomes enthusiastic over extraordinary-looking implement with Teeth, and does not consider quarter of an hour too long in

[5]

which to stand looking at it in silence. Feel that personally I have taken in the whole of its charms in something under six seconds—but do not, of course, say so. Fall instead into reverie about America, imagination runs away with me, and I die and am buried at sea before Robert says Well if I've had enough of the caterpillar—(caterpillar?)—What about some tea?

We accordingly repair to tea-tent—very hot and crowded, and benches show tendency to tip people off whenever other people get up. I drink strong tea and eat chudleighs, and cake with cherries in it. Small girl opposite, wedged in between enormous grandfather and grandfather's elderly friend, spills her tea, it runs down the table which is on a slope, and invades Robert's flannel trousers. He is not pleased, but says that It doesn't Matter, and we leave tent.

Meet contingent from our own village, exchange amiable observations, and Miss S. of the Post-Office draws me aside to ask if it is true that I am going to America? I admit that it is, and we agree that America is **A Long**

Way Off, with rider from Miss S. to the effect that she has a brother in Canada, he's been there for years and has a Canadian wife whom Miss S. has never seen, and further addition that things seem to be in a bad way there, altogether.

This interchange probably overheard by Robert, as he later in the evening says to me rather suddenly that he supposes this American business is really settled? I reply weakly that I suppose it is, and immediately add, more weakly still, that I can cancel the whole thing if he wants me to. To this Robert makes no reply whatever, and takes up *The Times*.

I listen for some time to unsympathetic female voice from the wireless, singing song that I consider definitely repellent about a forest, and address picture-postcards to Robin and Vicky at school, switch off wireless just as unsympathetic female branches off into something about wild violets, write list of clothes that I shall require for America, and presently discover that I have missed the nine o'clock news altogether. Robert also discovers this, and is again not pleased.

[7]

Go up to bed feeling discouraged and notice a smell in the bathroom, but decide to say nothing about it till morning. Robert, coming up hours later, wakes me in order to enquire whether I noticed anything when I was having my bath? Am obliged to admit that I did, and he says this means taking up the whole of the flooring, and he'll take any bet it's a dead rat. Do not take up this challenge as (a) he is probably right (b) I am completely sodden with sleep.

July 11th.—Car of extremely antiquated appearance rattles up to the door, and efficient-looking woman in grey trousers and a jumper gets out, evidently Mrs. Tressider. The Boy is shortly afterwards revealed, cowering amongst suit-cases, large kettle, portions of a camp-bed, folding rubber bath and case of groceries, in back of car. He looks pale and hunted, and is said to be fourteen, but seems to me more like ten. (Extra milk, however, almost certainly superfluous. *Mem:* tell Cook to use up for pudding to-night.)

Mrs. T. very brisk and talkative, says that she and The Boy are on their way to Wales,

[8]

The Boy is . . . revealed cowering amongst suit-cases

where they propose to camp. I hint that the holidays have begun early, and Mrs. T. shakes her head at me, frowns, hisses, and then says in a loud voice and with an unnatural smile, that The Boy hasn't been very strong and was kept at home last term but will be going back next, and what he'd love better than anything would be a ramble round my lovely garden.

Am well aware that this exercise cannot possibly take more than four-and-a-half minutes, but naturally agree, and The Boy disappears, looking depressed, in the direction of the pigsty.

Mrs. T. then tells me that he had a nervous breakdown not long ago, and that the school mismanaged him, and the doctor did him no good, and she is taking the whole thing into her own hands and letting him Run Wild for a time. (Should much like to enquire how she thinks he is to run wild on back-seat of car, buried under a mountain of luggage.)

She then admires the house, of which she hasn't seen more than the hall door, says that I am marvellous—(very likely I am, but not for any reason known to Mrs. T.)—and asks

[9]

if it is true that I am off to America? Before I know where I am, we are discussing this quite violently, still standing in the hall. Suggestion that Mrs. T. would like to go upstairs and take her hat off goes unheeded, so does appearance of Florence with kettle on her way to the dining-room. I keep my eye fixed on Mrs. T. and say Yes, Yes, but am well aware that Florence has seen grey trousers and is startled by them, and will quite likely give notice to-morrow morning.

Mrs. T. tells me about America—she knows New York well, and has visited Chicago, and once spoke to a Women's Luncheon Club in Boston, and came home *via* San Francisco and the Coast—and is still telling me about it when I begin, in despair of ever moving her from the hall, to walk upstairs. She follows in a sleep-walking kind of way, still talking, and am reminded of Lady Macbeth, acted by Women's Institute last winter.

Just as we reach top-landing, Robert appears in shirt-sleeves, at bathroom door, and says that *half* a dead rat has been found, and the other half can't be far off. Have only too much reason to think that this is probably true. Robert then sees Mrs. T., is introduced, but—rightly—does not shake hands, and we talk about dead rat until gong sounds for tea.

The Boy reappears—inclination to creep sideways, rather than walk, into the room—and Mrs. T. asks Has he been galloping about all over the place, and The Boy smiles feebly but says nothing, which I think means that he is avoiding the lie direct.

Mrs. T. reverts to America, and tells me that I must let my flat whilst I am away, and she knows the very person, a perfectly charming girl, who has just been turned out of Taviton Street. I say: Turned out of Taviton Street? and have vision of perfectly charming girl being led away by the police to the accompaniment of stones and brickbats flung by the more exclusive inhabitants of Taviton Street, but it turns out that no scandal is implied, lease of perfectly charming girl's flat in Taviton Street having merely come to an end in the ordinary way. She has, Mrs. T. says, absolutely *nowhere* to go. Robert suggests a Y.W.C.A. and I say what about the Salvation Army, but these pleasantries not a success, and Mrs. T. becomes earnest, and says that Caroline Concannon would be the *Ideal* tenant. Literary, intelligent, easy to get on with, absolutely independent, and has a job in Fleet Street. Conceive violent prejudice against C.C. on the spot, and say hastily that flat won't be available till I sail, probably not before the 1st October. Mrs. T. then extracts from me, cannot imagine how, that flat contains two rooms, one with sofa-bed, that I am not in the least likely to be there during the summer holidays, that it would Help with the Rent if I had a tenant during August and September, and finally that there is no sound reason why C. Concannon should not move in on the spot, provided I will post the keys to her at once and write full particulars. Robert tries to back me up by saying that the post has gone, but Mrs. T. is indomitable, and declares that she will catch it in the first town she comes to. She will also write to C.C. herself, and tell her what an Opportunity it all is. She then springs from the tea-table in search of writing materials, and Robert looks at me compassionately and walks out into the garden, followed at a distance by The Boy, who chews leaves as he goes, as if he hadn't had enough tea.

Feel worried about this, and suggest to Mrs. T. that Fabian doesn't look very strong, but she laughs heartily and replies that The Boy is one of the wiry sort, and it's against all her principles to worry. Should like to reply that I wish she would apply this rule to her concern about my flat—but do not do so. Instead, am compelled by Mrs. T. to write long letter to her friend, offering her every encouragement to become my tenant in Doughty Street.

This, when accomplished, is triumphantly put into her bag by Mrs. T. with the assurance that she is pretty certain it is going to be absolutely All Right. Feel no confidence that her definition of all-rightness will coincide with mine.

We then sit in the garden and she tells me about education, a new cure for hay-fever, automatic gear-changing, and books that she has been reading. She also asks about the children, and I say that they are at school, and she hopes

[13]

that the schools are run on New Thought lines
—but to this I can only give a doubtful affirma-
tive in Vicky's case and a definite negative in
Robin's. Mrs. T. shakes her head, smiles, and
says something of which I only hear the word
Pity. Feel sure that it will be of no use to
pursue this line any further, and begin firmly
to tell Mrs. T. about recent letter from Rose,
—but in no time we are back at education
again, and benefits that The Boy has derived
from being driven about the country tête-à-tête
with his parent. (Can only think that his previous state must have been deplorable indeed, if
this constitutes an improvement.)

Time goes on, Mrs. T. still talking, Robert
looks over box-hedge once and round may-tree
twice, but disappears again without taking action, The Boy remains invisible.

Gradually find that I am saying Yes and I
See at recurrent intervals, and that features
are slowly becoming petrified into a glare. Mrs.
T. fortunately appears to notice nothing, and
goes on talking. I feel that I am probably going
to yawn, and pinch myself hard, at the same
time clenching my teeth and assuming expres-

sion of preternatural alertness that I know to be wholly unconvincing. Mrs. T. still talking. We reach Caroline Concannon again, and Mrs. T. tells me how wonderfully fortunate I shall be if what she refers to—inaccurately—as "our scheme" materialises. Decide inwardly that I shall probably murder Caroline C. within a week of meeting her, if she has anything like the number of virtues and graces attributed to her by Mrs. T.

Just as I am repeating to myself familiar lines, frequently recurred to in similar situations, to the effect that Time and the hour ride through the roughest day, all is brought to an end by Mrs. T. who leaps to her feet—movements surely extraordinarily sudden and energetic for a woman of her age?—and declares that they really must be getting on.

The Boy is retrieved, Robert makes final appearance round may-tree, and we exchange farewells. (Mine much more cordial than is either necessary or advisable, entirely owing to extreme relief at approaching departure.)

Mrs. T. wrings my hand and Robert's, smiles and nods a good deal, says more about Caroline

[15]

Concannon and the flat, and gets into driving seat. The Boy is already crouching amongst luggage at the back, and car drives noisily away.

Robert and I look at one another, but are too much exhausted to speak.

July 17th.—Decide that I must go to London, interview Caroline Concannon, and collect Robin and Vicky, on their way home from school. I tell Robert this, and he says in a resigned voice that he supposes this American plan is going to Upset Everything—which seems to me both unjust and unreasonable. I explain at some length that Caroline C. has been foisted on me by Mrs. Tressider, that I have been in vigorous correspondence with her for days about the flat, and should like to bring the whole thing to an end, and that an escort for Vicky from London to Devonshire would have to be provided in any case, so it might just as well be me as anybody else. To all of this Robert merely replies, after some thought, that he always knew this American scheme would mean turning everything upside down,

[16]

Robert makes final appearance round may-tree

and he supposes we shall just have to put up with it.

Am quite unable to see that Robert has anything whatever to put up with at present, but realise that to say so will be of no avail, and go instead to the kitchen, where Cook begs my pardon, but it's all over the place that I'm off to America, and she doesn't know what to answer when people ask her about it. Nothing for it, evidently, but to tell Cook the truth, which I do, and am very angry with myself for apologetic note that I hear in my voice, and distinct sensation of guilt that invades me.

Cook does nothing to improve this attitude by looking cynically amused when I mutter something about my publisher having wished me to visit New York, and I leave the kitchen soon afterwards. Directly I get into the hall, remember that I never said anything about eggs recently put into pickle and that this has got to be done. Return to kitchen, Cook is in fits of laughter talking to Florence, who is doing nothing at the sink.

I say—O, Cook,—which is weak in itself, as an opening—deliver vacillating statement about eggs, and go away again quickly. Am utterly dissatisfied with my own conduct in this entire episode, and try to make up for it—but without success—by sharply-worded postcard to the newsagent, who never remembers to send *The Field* until it is a fortnight old.

July 20th.—Doughty Street. Am taken to the station and seen off by Robert, who refrains from further reference to America, and regain Doughty Street flat, now swathed in dust-sheets. Remove these, go out into Gray's Inn Road and buy flowers, which I arrange in sitting-room, also cigarettes, and then telephone to Miss Caroline Concannon in Fleet Street office. Fleet Street office replies austerely that if I will wait a minute I shall be Put Through, and a good deal of buzzing goes on. Draw small unicorn on blotting-pad while I wait. Another voice says Do I want Miss Concannon? Yes, I do. Then just one minute, please. At least three minutes elapse, and I draw rather good near-Elizabethan cottage, with shading. Resentfully leave this unfinished when C. Concannon at last attains the telephone and speaks to me. Voice sounds young and cheerful, nicer

[18]

than I expected. We refer to Mrs. Tressider, and recent correspondence, and agree that an early interview is desirable. Shall she, says Caroline C., come round at once in her tiny car? Nothing could be easier. Am much impressed (a) at her having a tiny car (b) at her being able to drive it in London (c) at the ease with which she can leave Fleet Street office to get on without her services.

Look round flat, which has suddenly assumed entirely degraded appearance, feel certain that she will despise both me and it, and hastily powder my nose and apply lip-stick. Fleeting fancy crosses my mind that it would look rather dashing, and perhaps impress C.C. if I put on last year's beach-pyjamas—red linen, with coffee-colored top—but courage fails me, and I remain as I am, in blue delaine, thirty-five shillings off the peg from Exeter High Street establishment.

Car is audible outside, I look from behind curtains and see smallest baby Austin in the world—(I should imagine)—draw up with terrific *verve* outside the door. Incredibly slim and smart young creature steps out—black and

[19]

white frock with frills, tiny little white hat well over one ear, and perfectly scarlet mouth. She is unfortunately inspired to look up at window just as I crane my neck from behind curtain, and am convinced that she has seen me perfectly well, and is—rightly—disgusted at exhibition of vulgar and undignified curiosity.

Bell rings—very autocratic touch, surely?— I open the door, and Miss C. comes in. Should be very sorry to think that I am dismayed solely because she is younger, smarter, and better-looking than I am myself.

Agreeable conversation ensues, C.C. proves easy and ready to talk, we meet on the subject of Mrs. Tressider—boy looks browbeaten, Mrs. T. altogether too breezy and bracing—and further discover that we both know, and rather admire, Pamela Pringle. What, I ask, is the latest about Pamela, of whom I have heard nothing for ages? Oh, don't I know? says Miss C. Not about the stock-exchange man, and how he put Pamela on to a perfectly good thing, and it went up and up, and Pamela sold out and went to Antibes on the proceeds, and had a most thrilling affair with a gigolo, and the

Stock-Exchange nearly went mad? At this I
naturally scream for details, which C.C. gives
me with immense enthusiasm.

We remain utterly absorbed for some time,
until at last I remember that the flat still has to
be inspected, and offer to show Miss C. round.
(This a complete farce, as she could perfectly
well show herself, in something under five
minutes.)

She says How lovely to everything, but
pauses in the bathroom, and I feel convinced
that she has a prejudice against the geyser. (It
would be even stronger if she knew as much
about this one as I do.) Silence continues until
I become unnerved, and decide that I must offer
to take something off the rent. Just as I am
getting ready to say so, C.C. suddenly utters:
to the effect that she would like me to call her
Caroline.

Am surprised, relieved, and rather gratified,
and at once agree. Request, moreover, seems to
imply that we are to see something of one another in the future, which I take it means that
she is prepared to rent the flat. Further conversation reveals that this is so, and that she is

to move in next week, on the understanding
that I may claim use of sofa-bed in sitting-room
if I wish to do so. C.C. handsomely offers to let
me have the bedroom, and take sofa herself, I
say No, No, and we part with mutual esteem
and liking.

Am much relieved, and feel that the least I
can do is to write and thank Mrs. Tressider, to
whom the whole thing is owing, but unaccount-
able reluctance invades me, and day comes to
an end without my having done so.

July 22nd.—Ring up dear Rose and consult
her about clothes for America. She says at once
that she knows the very person. A young man
who will one day be a second Molyneux. I
mustn't dream of going to anybody else. She
will send me the address on a postcard. She
also knows of a woman who makes hats, a remedy for sea-sickness, and a new kind of hair-
slide. I say Yes, and Thank you very much, to
everything, and engage to meet Rose for lunch
to-morrow at place in Charlotte Street where
she says elliptically that you can eat on the
pavement.

Just as I have hung up receiver, telephone

bell rings again and I find myself listening to
Mrs. Tressider. She has, she says, left The Boy
in Wales with his father—(never knew he
had one, and am startled)—and dashed up on
business for one night, but is dashing back
again to-morrow. She just wanted to say how
glad she was that Caroline and I have settled
about the flat. She always knew it was the ideal
arrangement for us both.

Experience instant desire to cancel deal with
Caroline C. on the spot, but do not give way to
it, and conversation ends harmoniously, with
promise from myself to let Mrs. T. know when
and in what ship I am sailing, as she thinks she
may be able to Do Something about it.

July 24th.—Arrival of Robin at Waterloo,
where I go to meet him and see customary collection of waiting parents, and think how de-
pressing they all look, and feel certain they
think exactly the same about me. Train is late,
as usual, and I talk to pale mother in beige coat
and skirt and agree that the boys all come back
looking very well, and that schools nowadays
are quite different, and children really adore
being there. After that she tells me that her

Peter hates games and is no good at lessons, and I say that my Robin has never really settled down at school at all, and we agree that boys are much more difficult than girls. (Shall not, however, be surprised, if I find occasion to reverse this dictum after a few days of dear Vicky's society at home.)

Train comes in, and parents, including myself, hurry madly up and down platform amongst shoals of little boys in red caps. Finally discover Robin, who has grown enormously, and is struggling under immensely heavy bag.

We get into a taxi, and dash to Poland Street, where Green Line 'bus deposits Vicky with suit-case—handle broken, and it has to be dragged—bulging hat-box, untidy-looking brown paper parcel, two books—*Micky Mouse Annual* and *David Copperfield*, which I think odd mixture—and half-eaten packet of milk chocolate.

She screams and is excited, and says she is hungry, and Robin supports her with assertion that he is absolutely starving, and we leave lug-

She screams and is excited, and says she is hungry

gage at depot and go and eat ices at establishment in Oxford Street.

Remainder of the day divided between shopping, eating, and making as much use as possible of underground moving stairway, for which R. & V. have a passion.

July 25th.—Telephone appeal from Caroline Concannon saying can she move into Doughty Street flat immediately, as this is the best day for the van. Am alarmed by the sound of the van, and ask if she has realised that the flat is furnished already, and there isn't much room to spare. Yes, she knows all that, and it's only one or two odds and ends, and if she may come round with a tape-measure, she can soon tell. Feel that this is reasonable and must be acceded to, and suggest to the children that they should play quietly with bricks in the bedroom. They agree to this very readily, and shortly afterwards I hear them playing, not quietly at all, with a cricket-ball in the kitchen.

Caroline Concannon arrives soon afterwards —velocity of tiny car, in relation to its size, quite overwhelming—and rushes into the flat. No sign of tape-measure, but the van, she says,

[25]

will be here directly. This proves to be only too true, and the van shortly afterwards appears, and unloads a small black wardrobe, a quantity of pictures—some of these very, very modern indeed and experience fleeting hope that the children will not insist on detailed examination but this probably old-fashioned and not to be encouraged—two chairs, at least seventeen cushions, little raffia footstool that I do not care about, plush dog with green eyes that I care about still less, two packing cases—probably china?—a purple quilt which is obviously rolled round a large number of miscellaneous objects, and a portmanteau that C.C. says is full of books. I ask What about her clothes, and she says, Oh, those will all come later with the luggage.

Am rather stunned by this, and take no action at all. C.C. is active and rushes about and shortly afterwards Robin and Vicky emerge from the kitchen and become active too. Small man materialises and staggers up and down stairs, carrying things, and appeals to me—as well he may—about where they are to go. I say Here, and What about *that* corner, as hopefully as possible, and presently find that all my own belongings are huddled together in the middle of the sitting-room, like survivors of a wreck clinging to a raft, while all C.C.'s goods and chattels are lined in rows against the walls.

C.C.—must remember to call her Caroline—is apologetic, and offers rather recklessly to take all her things away again if I like, but this is surely purely rhetorical, and I take little notice of it. At twelve o'clock she suddenly suggests that the children would like an ice, and rushes them away, and I am left feeling partly relieved at getting rid of them and partly agitated because it is getting so near lunch-time.

Make a few tentative efforts about furniture and succeed in clearing a gangway down the middle of sitting-room—this a definite improvement—but find increasing tendency to move everything that seems to be occupying too much space, into kitchen. Caroline has evidently had same inspiration, as I find small armchair there, unknown to me hitherto, standing on its head, two waste-paper baskets—(something tells me these are likely to be very much used in the near future)—large saucepan, oriental-looking drapery that might be a bedspread, and folded oak table that will not, to my certain knowledge, fit into any single room when extended.

Telephone bell interrupts me—just as well, as I am growing rather agitated—and Rose's voice enquires if I have done anything yet about my clothes for America. Well no, not so far, but I am really going to see about it in a day or two. Rose is, not unjustifiably, cynical about this, and says that she will herself make an appointment for me to-morrow afternoon. Can see no way of getting out of this, as Felicity Fairmead has offered to take children for the day, so as to set me free, and therefore can only acquiesce. Unescapable conviction comes over me that I shan't be able to find a complete set of undergarments that match, for when I have to be tried on—but perhaps this will only take place at a later stage? Must remember to bear the question in mind when dealing with laundry, but am aware that I have been defeated on the point before, and almost certainly shall be again.

Caroline Concannon returns with children,

we all go out together and have inexpensive lunch of fried fish, chipped potatoes and meringues at adjacent Lyons, after which there seems to be a general feeling that C.C. is one of ourselves, and both the children address her by her Christian name.

Am much struck by all of this, and decide that the Modern Girl has been maligned. Possible material here for interesting little article on Pre-conceived Opinions in regard to Unfamiliar Types? Have vague idea of making a few notes on these lines, but this finally resolves itself into a list of minor articles required by Robin and Vicky, headed, as usual, by Tooth Paste.

(*Query:* Do all schools possess a number of pupils whose parents are unable or unwilling to supply them with tooth paste, and are they accordingly invited to share that of the better-equipped? Can think of no other explanation for the permanently depleted state of tubes belonging to Robin and Vicky.)

August 15th.—Holidays rush by, with customary dizzying speed and extremely unusual number of fine days. We go for picnics—sugar is forgotten once, and salt twice—drive immense distances in order to bathe for ten minutes in sea, which always turns out cold—and Robin takes up tennis. Felicity Fairmead comes to stay, is as popular as ever with children, and more so than ever with Robert as she has begun to play the piano again, and does so whenever we ask her. This leads to successful musical evenings, except when I undertake to sing solo part of "Alouette" and break down rather badly. Make up for it—or so I think—by restrained, but at the same time moving, interpretation of "In the Gloaming." Felicity, however, says that it reminds her of her great-grandmother, and Robert enquires If that is what's-his-name's Funeral March? and I decide to sing no more for the present.

Caroline Concannon also honors us by weekend visit, and proves incredibly lively. Am led to ask myself at exactly what stage youth, in my own case, gave way to middle-age, and become melancholy and introspective. C.C. however, insists on playing singles with me at eleven o'clock in the morning, and showers extravagant praise on what she rightly describes as my *one* shot, and soon afterwards she suggests that we should all go in the car to the nearest confectioner's and get ices. Children are naturally enthusiastic, and I find myself agreeing to everything, including bathing-picnic in the afternoon.

This leads to complete neglect of household duties hitherto viewed as unescapable, also to piles of unanswered letters, unmended clothes, and total absence of fresh flowers indoors, but no cataclysmic results ensue, and am forced to the conclusion that I have possibly exaggerated the importance of these claims on my time hitherto.

Ask C.C. about the flat and she is airy, and says Oh, she hopes I won't think it too frightfully untidy—(am perfectly certain that I shall)—and she had a new washer put on the kitchen tap the other day, which she evidently thinks constitutes conclusive evidence as to her being solid and reliable tenant. She also adds that there is now a kitten in Doughty Street, practically next door, and that the chandelier needs cleaning but can only be done by A Man. Am struck, not for the first time, by the number

[31]

of contingencies, mostly of a purely domestic
character, that can apparently only be dealt
with by A Man.

August 31st.—Imperatively-worded postcard
from Mrs. Tressider informs me that I am to
write instantly to offices of the Holland-Amer-
ica Line, and book passage in *S.S.Rotterdam*,
sailing September 30th. If I do this, says postcard, very illegibly indeed, I shall be privileged
to travel with perfectly delightful American,
wife of well-known financier, and great friend
of Mrs. T's. Details will follow, but there is not
a moment to be lost. Am infected by this spirit
of urgency, write madly to the Holland-Amer-
ica Line, and then wonder—too late—whether
I really want to thrust my companionship on
perfectly delightful unknown American and—
still more—whether she will see any reason to
thank me for having done so. Letter, however,
arrives from shipping offices, enclosing enormous plan, entirely unintelligible to me, over
which Robert spends a good deal of time with
his spectacles on, and quantities of information
from which I extract tonnage of ship—which
leaves me cold—and price of single fare, which

is less than I expected, and reassures me. Robert says that he supposes this will do as well as anything else—not at all enthusiastically—and Vicky quite irrationally says that I *must* go in that ship and no other. (Disquieting thought: Will Vicky grow up into a second Mrs. T.? Should not be in the very least surprised if she did.)

Second postcard from Mrs. T. arrives: She has seen her American friend—(How?)—and the friend is absolutely delighted at the idea of travelling with me, and will do everything she can to help me. Idle impulse assails me to write back on another postcard and say that it would really help me more than anything if she would pay my passage for me—but this, naturally, dismissed at once. Further inspection of postcard, which is extensively blotted, reveals something written in extreme right-hand corner, of which I am unable to make out a word. Robert is appealed to, and says that he thinks it has something to do with luggage, but am quite unable to subscribe to this, and refer to Our Vicar's Wife, who has called in about morris-dancing. She says Yes, yes, where are her

[33]

glasses, and takes a good many things out of her bag and puts them all back again and finally discovers glasses in a little case in her bicycle basket, and studies postcard from a distance of at least a yard away.

Result of it all is that It Might be Anything, and Our Vicar's Wife always has said, and always will say, that plain sewing is a great deal more important than all this higher education. As for Our Vicar, says Our Vicar's Wife, he makes an absolute point of seeing that the Infant School is taught its multiplication-table in the good old-fashioned way.

We all agree that this is indeed essential, and conversation drifts off to Harvest Festival, drought in Cheshire—Our Vicar's married sister in despair about her French beans—tennis at Wimbledon, and increasing rarity of the buzzard-hawk.

Hours later, Robin picks up Mrs. T.'s postcard, and reads the whole of it from end to end, including postscript, to the effect that I must be prepared to pay duty on every single thing I take to America, especially anything new in the way of clothes. Am so much impressed by dear Robin's skill that I quite forget to point out utter undesirability of reading postcards addressed to other people till long after he has gone to bed.

Am much disturbed at the idea of paying duty on all my clothes, and lie awake for some time wondering if I can possibly evade obligations already incurred towards Rose's friend—the coming Molyneux—but decide that this cannot honorably be done.

September 1st.—Call upon aged neighbor, Mrs. Blenkinsop, to meet married-daughter Barbara Carruthers, newly-returned from India with baby. Find large party assembled, eight females and one very young man—said to be nephew of local doctor—who never speaks at all but hands tea about very politely and offers me dish containing swiss-roll no less than five times.

Barbara proves to have altered little, is eloquent about India, and talks a good deal about *tiffin*, also Hot Weather and Going up to the Hills. We are all impressed, and enquire after husband. He is, says Barbara, well, but he works too hard. Far too hard. She thinks that

[35]

he will kill himself, and is always telling him so.

Temporary gloom cast by the thought of Crosbie Carruthers killing himself is dissipated by the baby, who crawls about on the floor, and is said to be like his father. At this, however, old Mrs. Blenkinsop suddenly rebels, and announces that dear Baby is the image of herself as a tiny, and demands the immediate production of her portrait at four years old, to prove her words. Portrait is produced, turns out to be a silhouette, showing pitch-black little profile with ringlets and necklace, on white background, and we all say Yes, we quite see what she means.

Baby very soon afterwards begins to cry— can this be cause and effect?—and is taken away by Barbara.

Mrs. B. tells us that it is a great joy to have them with her, she has given up the whole of the top floor to them, and it means engaging an extra girl, and of course dear Baby's routine has to come before everything, so that her little house is upside-down—but that, after all, is nothing. She is old, her life is over, nothing

Old Mrs. Blenkinsop . . . announces that dear Baby
is the image of herself as a tiny

now matters to her, except the welfare and happiness of her loved ones.

Everybody rather dejected at these sentiments, and I seek to make a diversion by referring to approaching departure for America.

Several pieces of information are then offered to me:

The Americans are very hospitable.

The Americans are so hospitable that they work one to death. (Analogy here with Barbara's husband?)

The Americans like the English.

The Americans do not like the English at all.

It is not safe to go out anywhere in Chicago without a revolver. (To this I might well reply that, so far as I am concerned, it would be even less safe to go out with one.)

Whatever happens I must visit Hollywood, eat waffles, see a base-ball match, lunch at a Women's Club, go up to the top of the Woolworth Building, and get invited to the house of a millionaire so as to see what it's like.

All alcohol in America is wood-alcohol and if I touch it I shall die, or become blind or go raving mad.

It is quite impossible to refuse to drink alcohol in America, because the Americans are so hospitable.

Decide after this to go home, and consult Robert as to advisability of cancelling proposed visit to America altogether.

September 7th.—Instructions from America reach me to the effect that I am to stay at Essex House, in New York. Why Essex? Should much have preferred distinctive American name, such as Alabama or Connecticut House. Am consoled by enclosure, which gives photograph of superb skyscraper, and informs me that, if I choose, I shall be able to dine in the Persian Coffee Shop, under the direction of a French chef, graduate of the Escoffier School.

The English Molyneux sends home my clothes in instalments, am delighted with flowered red silk which is—I hope—to give me self-confidence in mounting any platform on which I may have the misfortune to find myself—also evening dress, more or less devoid of back, in very attractive pale brocade. Show red silk to Our Vicar's Wife, who says Marvellous, dear, but do not produce backless evening frock.

[38]

September 20th.—Letter arrives from complete stranger—signature seems to be Ella B. Chickhyde, which I think odd—informing me that she is so disappointed that the sailing of the *Rotterdam* has been cancelled, and we must sail instead by the *Statendam*, on October 7th, unless we like to make a dash for the *previous* boat, which means going on board the day after to-morrow, and will I be so kind as to telegraph? Am thrown into confusion by the whole thing, and feel that Robert will think it is all my fault—which he does, and says that Women Never Stick to Anything for Five Minutes Together—which is wholly unjust, but makes me feel guilty all the same. He also clears up identity of Ella B. Chickhyde, by saying that she must be the friend of that woman who came in a car on her way to Wales, and talked. This at once recalls Mrs. Tressider, and I telegraph to Ella B. Chickhyde to say that I hope to sail on the *Statendam*.

Last day of the holidays then takes its usual course, I pack frantically in the intervals of reading *Vice Versa* aloud, playing Corinthian Bagatelle, sanctioning an expedition to the vil-

[39]

lage to buy sweets, and helping Vicky over her holiday task, about which she has suddenly become acutely anxious, after weeks of brassy indifference.

September 21st.—Take children to London, and general dispersal ensues. Vicky drops large glass bottle of sweets on to platform at Waterloo, with resultant breakage, amiable porter rushes up and tells her not to cry, as he can arrange it all. This he does by laboriously separating broken glass from sweets, with coal-black hands, and placing salvage in a piece of newspaper. Present him with a florin, and am not sufficiently strong-minded to prevent Vicky from going off with newspaper parcel bulging in coat pocket.

Robin and I proceed to Charing Cross—he breaks lengthy silence by saying that to *him* it only seems one second ago that I was meeting him here, instead of seeing him off—and this moves me so much that I am quite unable to answer, and we walk down Platform Six—Special School-train—without exchanging a syllable. The place is, as usual, crowded with parents and boys, including minute creature who can scarcely be seen under grey wide-awake hat, and who I suggest must be a new boy. Robin, however, says Oh, no, that's *quite* an old boy, and seems slightly amused.

Parting, thanks to this blunder on my part, is slightly less painful than usual, and I immediately go and have my hair washed and set, in order to distract my thoughts, before proceeding to Doughty Street. Caroline awaits me there, together with lavish display of flowers that she has arranged in my honor, which touches me, and entirely compensates for strange disorder that prevails all over flat. Moreover, C.C. extraordinarily sweet-tempered and acquiesces with apologies when I suggest the removal of tiny green hat, two glass vases and a saucepan, from the bathroom.

September 25th.—Attend dinner-party of most distinguished people, given by celebrated young publisher connected with New York house. Evening is preceded by prolonged mental conflict on my part, concerning—as usual—clothes. Caroline C. urges me to put on new backless garment, destined for America, but superstitious feeling that this may be unlucky assails

[41]

me, and I hover frantically between very old blue and comparatively new black-and-white stripes. Caroline is sympathetic throughout, but at seven o'clock suddenly screams that she is due at a sherry party and must rush, she'd forgotten all about it.

(Extraordinary difference between this generation and my own impresses me immensely. Should never, at C.C.'s age—or probably any other—have forgotten even a tea-party, let alone a sherry one. This no time, however, for indulging in philosophical retrospective studies.)

Baby Austin, as usual, is at the door, C.C. leaps into it and vanishes, at terrific pace, into Guildford Street, leaving me to get into black-and-white stripes, discover that black evening shoes have been left at home, remember with relief that grey brocade ones are here and available, and grey silk stockings that have to be mended, but fortunately above the knee. Result of it all is that I am late, which I try to feel is modern, but really only consider bad-mannered.

Party is assembled when I arrive, am delighted to see Distinguished Artist, well-known

to me in Hampstead days, whom I at once perceive to have been celebrating the occasion almost before it has begun—also famous man of
letters next whom I am allowed to sit at dinner, and actor with whom I have—in common
with about ninety-nine per cent of the feminine
population—been in love for years. (This state
of affairs made much worse long before the end
of the evening.)

Party is successful from start to finish, everybody wishes me a pleasant trip to America, I
am profoundly touched and feel rather inclined
to burst into tears—hope this has nothing to
do with the champagne—but fortunately remember in time that a scarlet nose and patchy
face can be becoming to no one. (Marked dis-
crepancy here between convention so prevalent in fiction, and state of affairs common to
everyday life.)

Am escorted home at one o'clock by Distinguished Artist and extraordinarily pretty girl,
called Dinah, with dimple, and retire to sofa-
bed in sitting-room, taking every precaution
not to wake Caroline C., innocently slumbering
in bedroom.

[43]

Just as I have dropped asleep, hall-door bangs, and I hear feet rushing up the stairs, and wonder if it can be burglars, but decide that only very amateurish ones, with whom I could probably deal, would make so much noise. Point is settled by sudden appearance of light under bedroom door, and stifled, but merry, rendering of "Stormy Weather" which indicates that C.C. has this moment returned from belated revels no doubt connected with sherry party. Am impressed by this fresh evidence of the gay life lived by the young to-day, and go to sleep again.

October 1st.—Return home yesterday coincides with strong tendency to feel that I can't possibly go to America at all, and that most likely I shall never come back alive if I do, and anyway everything here will go to rack and ruin without me. Say something of these premonitions to Robert, who replies that (a) It would be great waste of money to cancel my passage now—(b) I shall be quite all right if I remember to look where I'm going when I cross the streets—and (c) he dares say Cook and Florence will manage very well. I ask wildly if he

[44]

will cable to me if anything goes wrong with
the children, and he says Certainly and enquires what arrangements I have made about
the servants' wages? Remainder of the evening
passes in domestic discussion, interrupted by
telephone call from Robert's brother William,
who says that he wishes to see me off at Southampton. Am much gratified by this, and think
it tactful not to enquire why dear William's
wife Angela has not associated herself with the
scheme.

October 7th.—Long and agitating day, of
which the close finds me on board S.S. *Statendam*, but cannot yet feel wholly certain
how this result has been achieved, owing to
confusion of mind consequent on packing, unpacking—for purpose of retrieving clothes-
brush and cheque-book, accidentally put in
twenty-four hours too early—consulting numbers of Lists and Notes, and conveying self and
luggage—six pieces all told, which I think
moderate—to boat-train at Waterloo.

Caroline Concannon has handsomely offered
to go with me to Southampton, and I have accepted, and Felicity Fairmead puts in unex-

[45]

pected and gratifying appearance at Waterloo. I say, Isn't she astonished to find me travelling first-class? and she replies No, not in the least, which surprises me a good deal, but decide that it's a compliment in its way.

Caroline C. and I have carriage to ourselves, but label on window announces that H. Press is to occupy Corner Seat, window side, facing engine. We decide that H.P. is evidently fussy, probably very old, and—says Caroline with an air of authority—most likely an invalid. The least we can do, she says, is to put all hand-luggage up on the rack and leave one side of carriage entirely free, so that he can put his feet up. Felicity says, Suppose he is lifted in on a wheel-chair? but this we disregard, as being mere conjecture. All, however, is wasted, as H. Press fails to materialise and train, to un-bounded concern of us all three, goes off with-out him.

Robert and William meet us at Southamp-ton, having motored from Devonshire and Wilt-shire respectively, and take us on board tender, where we all sit in a draught, on very hard seats. Robert shows me letters he has brought me from home—one from Our Vicar's Wife, full of good wishes very kindly expressed, and will I, if absolutely convenient, send photograph of Niagara Falls, so helpful in talking to school-children about wonders of Nature —the rest mostly bills. I tell Robert madly that I shall pay them all from America—which I know very well that I shan't—and we exchange comments, generally unfavorable, about fellow-passengers. Tender gets off at last —draught more pervasive than ever. Small steamers rise up at intervals, and Caroline says excitedly: There she is! to each of them. Enormous ship with four funnels comes into view, and *I* say: There she is! but am, as usual, wrong, and *Statendam* only reached hours later, when we are all overawed by her size, except Robert.

On board Robert takes charge of everything —just as well, as I am completely dazed—conducts us to Cabin 89, miraculously produces my luggage, tells me to have dinner and unpack the moment the tender goes off—(this advice surely strikes rather sinister note?)—and shows me where dining-saloon is, just as though he'd been there every day for years.

He then returns me to cabin, where William is quietly telling Caroline the story of his life, rings for steward and commands him to bring a bottle of champagne, and my health is drunk.

Am touched and impressed, and wonder wildly if it would be of any use to beg Robert to change all his plans and come with me to America after all? Unable to put this to the test, as bell rings loudly and dramatically, tender is said to be just off, and farewells become imminent. Robert, William and Caroline are urged by various officials to Mind their Heads, please, and Step this way—I exchange frantic farewells with all three, feel certain that I shall never see any of them again, and am left in floods of tears in what seems for the moment to be complete and utter solitude, but afterwards turns out to be large crowd of complete strangers, stewards in white jackets, and colossal palms in pots.

Can see nothing for it but to follow Robert's advice and go to dining-saloon, which I do, and find myself seated next to large and elderly

[48]

We are all overawed by her size, except Robert

American lady who works her way steadily through eight-course dinner and tells me that she is on a very strict diet. She also says that her cabin is a perfectly terrible one, and she knew the moment she set foot on the ship that she was going to dislike everything on board. She is, she says, like that. She always knows within the first two minutes whether she is going to like or dislike her surroundings. Am I, she enquires, the same? Should like to reply that it never takes me more than one minute to know exactly what I feel, not only about my surroundings, but about those with whom I have to share them. However, she waits for no answer, so this *mot*, as so many others, remains unuttered.

Friend of Mrs. Tressider, whom I have forgotten all about, comes up half-way through dinner, introduces herself as Ella Wheelwright —Chickhyde evidently a mistake—and seems nice. She introduces married sister and husband, from Chicago, and tells me that literary American, who says he has met me in London, is also on board. Would I like to sit at their table for meals? I am, however, to be perfectly honest about this. Am perfectly honest and say Yes, I should, but wonder vaguely what would happen if perfect honesty had compelled me to say No?

Elderly American lady seems faintly hurt at prospect of my desertion, and says resentfully how nice it is for me to have found friends, and would I like to come and look at her cabin? Question of perfect honesty not having here been raised, I do so, and can see nothing wrong with it whatever. Just as I am leaving it— which I do as soon as civility permits—see that name on door is H. Press. Must remember to send Felicity and Caroline postcards about this.

October 9th.—Interior of my own cabin becomes extremely familiar, owing to rough weather and consequent collapse. Feel that I shall probably not live to see America, let alone England again.

October 11th.—Emerge gradually from very very painful state of affairs. New remedy for sea-sickness provided by Rose may or may not be responsible for my being still alive, but that is definitely the utmost that can be said for it.

Remain flat on my back, and wish that I

could either read or go to sleep, but both
equally impossible. Try to recall poetry, by
way of passing the time, and find myself involved in melancholy quotations: "Sorrow's
crown of sorrows is remembering happier times"
alternating with "A few more years shall roll."
Look at snapshots of Robert and the children,
but this also a failure, as I begin to cry and
wonder why I ever left them. Have died and
been buried at sea several times before evening
and— alternatively—have heard of fatal accident to Robin, dangerous illness of Vicky, and
suicide of Robert, all owing to my desertion.
Endless day closes in profound gloom and renewed nausea.

October 12th.—Situation improved, I get up
and sit on deck, eat raw apples for lunch, and
begin to feel that I may, after all, live to see
America. Devote a good deal of thought, and
still more admiration, to Christopher Columbus
who doubtless performed similar transit to
mine, under infinitely more trying conditions.

Ella Wheelwright comes and speaks to me—
she looks blooming in almond-green dress with
cape, very smart—and is compassionate. We

[51]

talk about Mrs. Tressider—a sweet thing, says Ella W., and I immediately acquiesce, though description not in the least applicable, to my way of thinking—and agree that The Boy does not look strong. (Perceive that this is apparently the only comment that ever occurs to anybody, in connection with The Boy, and wonder if he is destined to go through life with this negative reputation and no other.)

Just as I think it must be tea-time, discover that all ship clocks differ from my watch, and am informed by deck-steward that The Time Goes Back an Hour every night. Pretend that I knew this all along, and had merely forgotten it, but am in reality astonished, and wish that Robert was here to explain.

Day crawls by slowly, but not too unpleasantly, and is enlivened by literary American, met once before in London, who tells me all about English authors in New York, and gives me to understand that, if popular, they get invited to cocktail-parties two or three times daily, and if unpopular, are obliged to leave the country.

October 14th.—America achieved. Statue of Liberty, admirably lit up, greets me at about seven o'clock this evening, entrance to harbor is incredibly beautiful and skyscrapers prove to be just as impressive as their reputation, and much more decorative.

Just as I am admiring everything from top-deck, two unknown young women suddenly materialise (risen from the ocean, like Venus?) —also young man with camera, and I am approached and asked if I will at once give my views on The United States, the American Woman, and Modern American Novels. Young man says that he wishes to take my photograph, which makes me feel like a film-star—appearance, unfortunately, does nothing to support this illusion—and this is duly accomplished, whilst I stand in *dégagé* attitude, half-way down companion-ladder on which I have never before set foot throughout the voyage.

Exchange farewells with fellow-passengers —literary American, now known to me as Arthur, is kindness itself and invites me on behalf of his family to come and visit them in Chicago and see World's Fair—Ella Wheelwright also kind and gives me her card, but obviously much preoccupied with question of Customs—as well she may be, as she informs me that she has declared two hundred dollars' worth of purchases made in Europe and has another five hundred dollars' worth undeclared.

American publisher has come to meet me and is on the dock. I am delighted to see him, and we sit on a bench for about two hours, surrounded by luggage, none of which seems to be mine. Eventually, however, it appears—which slightly surprises me—publisher supports me through Customs inspection and finally escorts me personally to Essex House, where I am rung up five times before an hour has elapsed, with hospitable greetings and invitations. (Nothing from Ella Wheelwright, and cannot help wondering if she has perhaps been arrested?)

Am much impressed by all of it, including marvellous view from bedroom on sixteenth storey, but still unable to contemplate photographs of children with complete calm.

October 16th.—Come to the conclusion that everything I have ever heard or read about American Hospitality is an understatement.

Telephone bell rings incessantly from nine
o'clock onward, invitations pour in, and complete strangers ring up to say that they liked
my book and would be glad to give a party for
me at any hour of the day or night. Am plunged
by all this into a state of bewilderment, but
feel definitely that it will be a satisfaction to
let a number of people at home hear about it
all, and realise estimation in which professional writers are held in America.

(Second thought obtrudes itself here, to the
effect that, if I know anything of my neighbors, they will receive any such information
with perfect calm and probably say Yes,
they've always heard that Americans were Like
That.)

Am interviewed by reporters on five different
occasions—one young gentleman evidently
very tired, and droops on a sofa without saying
much, which paralyses me and results in long
stretches of deathly silence. Finally he utters,
to the effect that John Drinkwater was difficult
to interview. Experience forlorn gleam of gratification at being bracketed with so distinguished a writer, but this instantly extin-

guished, as reporter adds that in the end, J.D. talked for one hour and fifteen minutes. Am quite unable to emulate this achievement, and interview ends in gloom. Representative of an evening paper immediately appears but is a great improvement on his colleague, and restores me to equanimity.

Three women reporters follow—am much struck by the fact that they are all good-looking and dress nicely—they all ask me what I think of the American Woman, whether I read James Branch Cabell—which I don't—and what I feel about the Problem of the Leisured Woman. Answer them all as eloquently as possible and make mental note to the effect that I have evidently never taken the subject of Women seriously enough, the only problem about them in England being why there are so many.

Lunch with distinguished publisher and his highly decorative wife and two little boys. Am not in the least surprised to find that they live in a flat with black velvet sofas, concealed lighting, and three diagonal glass tables for sole furniture. It turns out, however, that this is *not* a typical American home, and that they find it nearly as remarkable as I do myself. We have lunch, the two little boys behave like angels—reputation of American children evidently libellous, and must remember to say so when I get home—and we talk about interior decoration—dining-room has different colored paint on each one of its four walls— books, and sea-voyages. Elder of the two little boys suddenly breaks into this and remarks that he just loves English sausages— oh boy!—which I accept as a compliment to myself, and he then relapses into silence. Am much impressed by this display of social competence, and feel doubtful whether Robin or Vicky could ever have equalled it.

Afternoon is spent, once more, in interviews, and am taken out to supper-party by Ella Wheelwright, who again appears in clothes that I have never seen before. At supper I sit next elderly gentleman wearing collar exactly like Mr. Gladstone's. He is slightly morose, tells me that times are not at all what they were—which I know already—and that there is No Society any more, left in New York. This seems to me uncivil, as well as ungrateful, and I decline to assent. Elderly Gentleman is, however, entirely indifferent as to whether I agree with him or not, and merely goes on to say that no club would dream of admitting Jews to its membership. (This, if true, reflects no credit on clubs.) It also appears that, in his own house, cocktails, wireless, gramophones and modern young people are—like Jews—never admitted. Should like to think of something really startling to reply to all this, but he would almost certainly take no notice, even if I did, and I content myself with saying that that is Very Interesting—which is not, unfortunately, altogether true.

Ella Wheelwright offers to drive me home, which she does with great competence, though once shouted at by a policeman who tells her: Put your lights on, sister!

Ella is kind, and asks me to tell her all about my home, but follows this up by immediately telling me all about hers instead. She also invites me to two luncheons, one tea, and to spend Sunday with her on Long Island.

Return to my room, which is now becoming

familiar, and write long letter to Robert, which makes me feel homesick all over again.

October 17th.—Conference at publishers' office concerning my future movements, in which I take passive, rather than active, part. Head of well-known lecture agency is present, and tells me about several excellent speaking-engagements that he might have got for me if: (a) He had had longer notice (b) All the Clubs in America hadn't been affected by the depression and (c) I could arrange to postpone my sailing for another three months.

Since (a) and (b) cannot now be remedied, and I entirely refuse to consider (c) deadlock appears to have been reached, but agent suddenly relents and admits he *can*, by dint of superhuman exertions, get me one or two bookings in various places that none of them seem to be less than eighteen hours' journey apart. I agree to everything, only stipulating for Chicago, where I wish to visit literary friend Arthur and his family, and to inspect the World's Fair.

Social whirl, to which I am by now becoming accustomed, follows, and I am put into the

[59]

hands of extraordinarily kind and competent guardian angel, picturesquely named Ramona Herdman, who takes me to the Vanderbilt Hotel, for so-called tea, which consists of very strong cocktails and interesting sandwiches. I meet Mrs. Isabel Paterson, by whom I am completely fascinated but also awe-stricken in the extreme, as she has terrific reputation as a critic and is alarmingly clever in conversation.

She demolishes one or two English novelists in whose success I have always hitherto believed implicitly, but is kind about my own literary efforts, and goes so far as to hope that we shall meet again. I tell her that I am going to Chicago and other places and may be lecturing, and she looks at the floor and says, Yes, Clubwomen, Large women with marcelled hair, wearing reception gowns.

Am appalled by this thumbnail sketch and seriously contemplate cancelling tour altogether.

Ella Wheelwright joins us. She now has on a black ensemble and hair done in quite a new way, and we talk about books. I say that I have enjoyed nothing so much as *Flush*, but Mrs.

Paterson again disconcerts me by muttering that to write a whole book about a dog is Simply Morbid.

Am eventually taken to Essex House by Ella W. who asks, very kindly, if there is anything she can do for me. Yes, there is. She can tell me where I can go to get my hair shampooed and set, and whether it will be much more expensive than it is at home. In reply Ella tells me that her own hair waves naturally. It doesn't *curl*—that isn't what she means at all —but it just waves. In damp weather it just goes into natural waves. It always has done this ever since she was a child. But she has it set once a month because it looks nicer. Hairdresser always tells her that it's lovely hair to do anything with because the wave is really natural.

She then says good-night and leaves me, and I decide to have my own inferior hair, which does *not* wave naturally, washed and set in the hotel beauty-parlor.

October 23rd.—Extraordinary week-end with Ella Wheelwright on Long Island, at superb country-house which she refers to as her cottage. She drives me out from New York very kindly, but should enjoy it a great deal more if she would look in front of her, instead of at me, whilst negotiating colossal and unceasing stream of traffic. This, she says gaily, is what she has been looking forward to—a really undisturbed tête-à-tête in which to hear all about my reactions to America and the American Woman. I say, What about the American Man? But this not a success, Ella evidently feeling that reactions, if any, on this subject are of no importance whatever to anybody.

She then tells me that she spent a month last year in London staying at the Savoy, and gives me her opinion of England, which is, on the whole, favorable. I say at intervals that I see what she means, and utter other noncommittal phrases whenever it occurs to me that if I don't say something, she will guess that I am not really listening.

We gradually leave New York behind and get into comparative country—bright golden trees excite my admiration, together with occasional scarlet ones—Ella still talking—have not the least idea what about, but continue to ejaculate from time to time. Presently country

It doesn't curl—*that isn't what she means at all—but it just waves*

mansion is reached, three large cars already standing in front of door, and I suggest that other visitors have arrived, but Ella says Oh, no, one is her *other* car, and the remaining two belong to Charlie. Decide that Charlie must be her husband, and wonder whether she has any children, but none have ever been mentioned, and do not like to ask.

House is attractive—furniture and decorations very elaborate—am particularly struck by enormous pile of amber beads coiled carelessly on one corner of old oak refectory table, just where they catch the light—and I am taken up winding staircase carpeted in rose color.

(Evidently no children, or else they use a separate staircase.)

Ella's bedroom perfectly marvellous. Terrific expanse of looking-glass, and sofa has eighteen pillows, each one different shade of purple. Should like to count number of jars and bottles—all with mauve enamel tops—in bathroom, but this would take far too long, and feel it necessary, moreover, to concentrate on personal appearance, very far from satisfactory. Am aware that I cannot hope to compete

[63]

with Ella, who is looking wonderful in white wool outfit obviously made for her in Paris, but make what efforts I can with powder and lip-stick, try to forget that I am wearing my Blue, which never has suited me and utterly refuses to wear out. Decide to take off my hat, but am dissatisfied with my hair when I have done so, and put it on again and go downstairs. Complete house-party is then revealed to me, sitting on silk cushions outside French windows, the whole thing being entirely reminiscent of illustrations to society story in American magazine. I am introduced, everyone is very polite, and complete silence envelops the entire party.

Young man in white sweater at last rises to the occasion and asks me what I think of *Anthony Adverse*. Am obliged to reply that I haven't read it, which gets us no farther. I then admire the trees, which are beautiful, and everybody looks relieved and admires them too, and silence again ensues.

Ella, with great presence of mind, says that it is time for cocktails; these are brought, and I obediently drink mine and wonder what Our

Vicar's Wife would say if she could see me now. This leads, by natural transition, to thoughts of television, and I ask my neighbor —grey flannels and flaming red hair—whether he thinks that this will ever become part of everyday life. He looks surprised—as well he may—but replies civilly that he doubts it very much. This he follows up by enquiring whether I have yet read *Anthony Adverse.*

Charlie materialises—imagine him to be Ella's husband, but am never actually told so —and we all go in to lunch, which is excellent.

(Standard of American cooking very, very high indeed. Reflect sentimentally that Robert is, in all probability, only having roast beef and Yorkshire pudding, then remember difference in time between here and England, and realise that beef and Yorkshire pudding are either in the past or the future, although cannot be quite sure which.)

Tennis is suggested for the afternoon, and Ella tells me that she can easily find me a pair of shoes. As I am far from sharing this confidence—every other woman in the room looks like size 5, whereas I take 6 and a half—and think my Blue very ill-adapted to the tennis-court, I say that I would rather look on, and this I do. They all play extremely well and look incredibly handsome, well-dressed, and athletic. I decide, not for the first time, that Americans are a great deal more decorative than Europeans.

Just as inferiority complex threatens to overwhelm me altogether, I am joined by Ella, who says that she is taking me to a tea-party. Tea-parties are A Feature of Life on Long Island, and it is essential, says Ella, that I should attend one.

Everybody else turns out to be coming also, a complete platoon of cars is marshalled and we drive off, about two people to every car, and cover total distance of rather less than five hundred yards.

Am by this time becoming accustomed to American version of a tea-party, and encounter cocktails and sandwiches with equanimity, but am much struck by scale on which the entertainment is conducted; large room being entirely filled by people, including young gentleman who is playing the piano violently and has

extremely pretty girl on either side of him, each
with an arm round his waist.

It now becomes necessary to screech at really
terrific pitch and this everyone does. Cannot
feel that *Anthony Adverse motif*, which still
recurs, has gained by this, nor do my own replies to questions concerning the length of my
stay, my reactions to America, and opinion of
the American Woman. Ella, who has heroically
introduced everybody within sight, smiles and
waves at me encouragingly, but is now too
firmly wedged in to move, and I sit on a sofa,
next to slim woman in scarlet, and she screams
into my ear.

Am obliged to give up all hope of hearing
everything she says, but can catch quite a lot
of it, and am interested. She tells me that she
is a Southerner and was the mascot of the base-
ball team at her College in the South. Whenever a match took place, she was carried on
to the field by two members of the team.
(Frightful vision assails me of similar extrava-
gance taking place on village football-ground
at home, and results, especially as to mud and
bruises, that would certainly ensue.) On one

occasion, yells my neighbor, the opposing team objected to her presence—(am not surprised) —but her Boys held firm. Either, said her Boys, they had their mascot on the field, or else the whole match must be called off.

Cannot, unfortunately, hear the end of the story, but feel certain that it was favorable to the mascot and her Boys. Experience temporary difficulty in thinking out reasonably polite answer to such a singular statement, and finally say that it must have been rather fun, which is weak, and totally untrue, at least as far as the teams were concerned—but as all is lost in surrounding noise, it matters little. People walk in and out, and scream at one another—should be interested to identify my host and hostess, but see no hope of this whatever. Ella presently works her way up to me and makes signs that she is ready to leave, and we struggle slowly into the air again.

Remaining members of Ella's house-party, whom I am now rather disposed to cling to, as being old and familiar friends, all gradually reassemble, and we return to Ella's house,

where I discover that recent vocal efforts have
made my throat extremely sore.

October 25th.—English mail awaits me on return to New York hotel and is handed to me
by reception-clerk with agreeable comment to
the effect that the Old Country hasn't forgotten me *this* time. Feel that I can't possibly wait
to read mail till I get upstairs, but equally impossible to do so in entrance hall, and am prepared to make a rush for the elevator when
firm-looking elderly woman in black comes up
and addresses me by name. Says that she is very
glad indeed to know me. Her name is Katherine Ellen Blatt, which may not mean anything
to me, but stands for quite a lot to a section of
the American public.

I try to look intelligent and wonder whether
to ask for further details or not, but something
tells me that I am going to hear them anyway,
so may as well make up my mind to it. Invite
Miss Blatt to sit down and wait for me one
moment whilst I go up and take off my hat—
by which I really mean tear open letters from
Robert and the children—but she says, No,
she'd just love to come right upstairs with me.

This she proceeds to do and tells me on the way up that she writes articles for the women's magazines and that she makes quite a feature of describing English visitors to America, especially those with literary interests. The moment she heard that I was in New York she felt that she just had to come round right away and have a look at me—(idea crosses my mind of replying that A Cat may look at a King, but this colloquialism probably unappreciated, and in any case Miss B. gives me no time).

Bed still unmade, which annoys me, especially as Miss B. scrutinises entire room through a pince-nez and asks, What made me come here, as this is a place entirely frequented by professional people? She herself could, if I wish it, arrange to have me transferred immediately to a women's club, where there is a lovely group of highly intelligent cultivated women, to which she is proud to say that she belongs. Can only hope that my face doesn't reflect acute horror that invades me at the idea of joining any group of women amongst whom is to be numbered Miss Blatt.

Incredibly tedious half-hour ensues. Miss B.

*But she says, No, she'd just love to come right up-
stairs with me*

has a great deal to say, and fortunately seems
to expect very little answer, as my mind is entirely fixed on letters lying unopened in my
handbag. She tells me, amongst other things,
that Noel Coward, Somerset Maugham—
whom she calls "Willie," which I think pro-
fane—the Duchess of Atholl, Sir Gerald du
Maurier and Miss Amy Johnson are all very
dear friends of hers, and she would never
dream of letting a year pass without going to
England and paying each of them a visit. I say
rather curtly that I don't know any of them,
and add that I don't really feel I ought to take
up any more of Miss Blatt's time. That, declares Miss Blatt, doesn't matter at all. I'm not
to let that worry me for a moment. To hear
about dear old London is just everything to
her, and she is just crazy to be told whether I
know her close friends, Ellen Wilkinson, Re-
becca West, Nancy Astor and Ramsay Mac-
donald. Frantic impulse assails me and I say,
No, but that the Prince of Wales is a great
friend of mine. Is that so? returns Miss Blatt
quite unmoved. She herself met him for the
first time last summer at Ascot and they had

quite a talk. (If this really true can only feel perfectly convinced that any talk there was emanated entirely from Miss B.)

Just as I feel that the limits of sanity have been reached telephone bell rings and I answer it and take complicated message from Lecture Agent about Buffalo, which at first I think to be Natural History, but afterwards realise is a town.

Continuity of atmosphere is now destroyed and I remain standing and inform Miss Blatt that I am afraid that I shall have to go out. She offers to take me uptown, and I thank her and say No. Then, she says, it won't be any trouble to take me downtown. This time I say No without thanking her.

We spend about ten minutes saying good-bye. Miss Blatt assures me that she will get in touch with me again within a day or two, and meanwhile will send me some of her articles to read, and I finally shut the door on her and sit down on the bed, after locking the door for fear she should come back again.

Tear open letters from Robert and the children, read them three times at least, become homesick and rather agitated, and then read them all over again. Robert says that he will be glad when I get home again (am strongly tempted to book my passage for to-morrow) and adds details about the garden. Our Vicar, he adds, preached quite a good sermon on Sunday last, and Cook's sponge-cake is improving. Vicky's letter very affectionate, with rows of kisses and large drawing of a horse with short legs and only one visible ear. The Literary Society at school, writes Vicky, is reading Masefield, and this she enjoys very much. Am a good deal impressed and try to remember what I know of Masefield's work and how much of it is suitable for nine years old.

Robin's letter, very long and beautifully written, contains urgent request for any American slang expressions that I may meet with, but it must be *new* slang. Not, he explicitly states, words like Jake and Oke, which everybody knows already. He also hopes that I am enjoying myself and have seen some gangsters. A boy called Saunders is now reading a P. G. Wodehouse book called *Love Among the Chickens*. A boy called Badger has had his

front-tooth knocked out. There isn't, says
Robin in conclusion, much to write about, and
he sends Best Love.

Receive also charming letter from Caroline
Concannon, who says, gratifyingly, that she
misses me, and adds in a vague way that everything is All Right in the flat. Remaining
correspondence mostly bills, but am quite unable to pay any attention to them for more
reasons than one, and merely put them all together in an elastic band and endorse the top
one "Bills," which makes me feel businesslike
and practically produces illusion of having paid
them already.

Extraordinary feeling of exhaustion comes
over me, due partly to emotion and partly to
visit of Miss Katherine Ellen Blatt, and I decide to go out and look at shop-windows on
Fifth Avenue, which I do, and enjoy enormously.

Later in the day am conducted to a Tea—
cocktails and sandwiches as usual. Meet distinguished author and critic, Alexander Woollcott, who is amusing and talks to me very
kindly. In the middle of it telphone bell rings

and he conducts conversation with—presumably—an Editor, in which he says, No, no, he must positively decline to undertake any more work. The terms, he admits, are wonderful, but it simply can't be done. No, he can't possibly reconsider his decision. He has had to refuse several other offers of the same kind already. He can undertake nothing more. On this he rings off and resumes conversation just as if nothing had happened. Am completely lost in awe and admiration.

October 26th.—Telephone message reaches me just as I am contemplating familiar problem of packing more into suit-cases, hat-box and attaché case than they can possibly contain. Will I at once get into touch with Mrs. Margery Brown, who has received a letter about me from Mrs. Tressider in England. Conviction comes over me in a rush that I cannot and will not do anything of the kind, and I go on packing.

Telephone bell rings—undoubtedly Mrs. Margery Brown—and I contemplate leaving it unanswered, but am mysteriously unable to do so. Decide to pretend that I am my Secretary and say that I've gone out. Do so, but find my-self involved in hideous and unconvincing mud-dle, in which all pronouns become badly mixed up. Discover, moreover, after some moments, that I am not talking to Mrs. Margery Brown at all, but to unknown American lady who re-peats patiently that an old friend wishes to come round and see me. Name of old friend is unintelligible to me throughout, but finally I give way and say Very well, I shall be here for another hour before starting for Chicago.

(Am not, in actual point of fact, departing for Chicago until tonight. *Query:* Would it not, when time permits, be advisable to concentrate very seriously on increasing tendency to distort the truth to my own convenience? *Ans.:* Ad-visable, perhaps, but definitely un-nerving, and investigation probably better postponed until safely returned to home surroundings. Cannot wholly escape the suspicion that moral stand-ards are largely dependent upon geographical surroundings.)

Return to suit-cases, and decide that if bottle of witch-hazel is rolled in paper it can perfectly well be placed inside bedroom slipper, and that it will make all the difference if I remove bulky evening wrap from its present corner of suitcase, and bestow it in the bottom of hat-box. Result of these manœuvres not all I hope, as situation of best hat now becomes precarious, and I also suddenly discover that I have forgotten to pack photographs of Robin and Vicky, small red travelling clock, and pair of black shoes that are inclined to be too tight and that I never by any chance wear.

Despair invades me and I am definitely relieved when knock at the door interrupts me. I open it and am greeted by a scream:—*Ah, madame, quelle émotion!*—and recognise Mademoiselle. She screams again, throws herself into my arms, says *Mon Dieu, je vais me trouver mal, alors?* and sinks on to the bed, but does not cease to talk. She is, she tells me, with *une famille très américaine—assez comme-il-faut*—(which I think an ungenerous description)—and has promised to remain with them in New York for six months, at the end of which they are going to Paris, where she originally met them. Are they nice, and is Mademoiselle happy? I enquire. To this Mademoiselle can only throw up her hands, gaze at the ceiling, and exclaim that *le bonheur* is *bien peu de chose*—with which I am unable to agree. She further adds that never, for one moment, day or night, does she cease to think of *ce cher petit chez-nous du Devonshire* and *cet amour de Vicky*.

(If this is literally true, Mademoiselle cannot possibly be doing her duty by her present employers. Can also remember distinctly many occasions on which Mademoiselle, in Devonshire, wept and threw herself about in despair, owing to alleged dullness of the English countryside, insults heaped upon her by the English people, and general *manque de cœur et de délicatesse* of my own family, particularly Vicky.)

All, however, is now forgotten, and we indulge in immense and retrospective conversation in which Mademoiselle goes so far as to refer sentimentally to *ces bons jeux de cricket dans le jardin*. Do not, naturally, remind her of the number of times in which *ces bons jeux* were brought to an abrupt end by Mademoiselle herself flinging down her bat and walking

[78]

Le bonheur is bien peu de chose

away saying *Moi, je ne joue plus*, owing to having been bowled out by Robin.

She inspects photographs of the children and praises their looks extravagantly, but on seeing Robert's only observes resentfully *Tiens! on dirait qu'il a vieillit!* She then looks piercingly at me, and I feel that only politeness keeps her from saying exactly the same thing about me, so turn the conversation by explaining that I am packing to go to Chicago.

Packing! exclaims Mademoiselle. *Ah, quelle horreur! Quelle façon de faire les choses!* At this she throws off black kid gloves, small fur jacket, three scarves, large amethyst brooch, and mauve wool cardigan, and announces her intention of packing for me. This she does with extreme competence and unlimited use of tissue paper, but exclaims rather frequently that my folding of clothes is enough to *briser le cœur*.

I beg her to stay and have lunch with me, and she says *Mais non, mais non, c'est trop*, but is finally persuaded, on condition that she may take down her hair and put it up again before going downstairs. To this I naturally agree, and Mademoiselle combs her hair and declares that it reminds her of *le bon temps passé.*

Find it impossible to extract from her any coherent impressions of America as she only replies to enquiries by shaking her head and saying *Ah, l'Amérique, l'Amérique! C'est toujours le dollarrr, n'est-ce-pas?* Decide, however, that Mademoiselle has on the whole met with a good deal of kindness, and is in receipt of an enormous salary.

We lunch together in Persian Coffee Shop, Mademoiselle talking with much animation, and later she takes her departure on the understanding that we are to meet again before I sail.

Send hurried postcards of Tallest Building in New York to Robin and Vicky respectively, tip everybody in Hotel who appears to expect it, and prepare myself for night journey to Chicago.

October 27th.—Remember, not without bitterness, that everybody in England has told me that I shall find American trains much too hot, Our Vicar's Wife—who has never been to America—going so far as to say that a temperature of 100 degrees is quite usual. Find myself, on the contrary, distinctly cold, and am not in the least surprised to see snow on the ground as we approach Chicago.

Postcards of the World's Fair on sale in train, mostly colored very bright blue and very bright yellow. I buy one of the Hall of Science —suitable for Robert—Observation Tower— likely to appeal to Robin—Pre-historic Animals —Vicky—and Streets of Paris, which has a sound of frivolity that I think will please Caroline Concannon. Rose and Felicity get Avenue of Flags and Belgian Village respectively, because I have nothing else left. Inscribe various rather illegible messages on all these, mostly to the effect that I am enjoying myself, that I miss them all very much, and that I haven't time to write more just now, but will do so later.

Breakfast is a success—expensive, but good —and I succeed in attaining a moderate cleanliness of appearance before train gets in. Customary struggle with suit-case ensues—pyjamas and sponge-bag shut in after prolonged efforts, and this achievement immediately followed by

[81]

discovery that I have forgotten to put in brush-and-comb. At this colored porter comes to my rescue, and shortly afterwards, Chicago is reached.

Literary friend Arthur has not only gratifyingly turned up to meet me, but has brought with him very pretty younger sister, visiting friend from New York (male) and exclusive-looking dachshund, referred to as Vicki Baum.

Moreover, representative from publishers puts in an appearance—hat worn at a very dashing angle—know him only as Pete and cannot imagine how I shall effect introductions, but this fortunately turns out to be unnecessary.

Am rather moved at finding that both Arthur and Pete now appear to me in the light of old and dear friends, such is my satisfaction at seeing faces that are not those of complete strangers.

Someone unknown takes a photograph, just as we leave station— This, says Arthur impressively, hasn't happened since the visit of Queen Marie of Roumania—and we drive off.

Chicago strikes me as full of beautiful buildings, and cannot imagine why nobody ever says anything about this aspect of it. Do not like to ask anything about gangsters, and see no signs of their activities, but hope these may be revealed later, otherwise children will be seriously disappointed. The lake, which looks to me exactly like the sea, excites my admiration, and building in which Arthur's family lives turns out to be right in front of it.

They receive me in kindest possible manner —I immediately fall in love with Arthur's mother—and suggest, with the utmost tact, that I should like a bath at once. (After one look in the glass, can well understand why this thought occurred to them.)

Perceive myself to be incredibly dirty, dishevelled, and out of repair generally, and do what I can, in enormous bedroom and bathroom, to rectify this. Hair, however, not improved by my making a mistake amongst unaccustomed number of bath-taps and giving myself quite involuntary shower.

October 30th.—Feel quite convinced that I have known Arthur, his family, his New York friend, and his dog, all my life. They treat me with incredible kindness and hospitality and introduce me to all their friends.

Some of the friends—but not all—raise the Problem of the American Woman. Find myself as far as ever from having thought out intelligent answer to this and have serious thoughts of writing dear Rose and asking her to cable reply if Problem is to pursue me wherever I go in the United States.

Enormous cocktail-party is given by Arthur's mother, entirely in honor of New York friend —whom I now freely address as Billy—and myself. Bond of union immediately established between us, as we realise joint responsibility of proving ourselves worthy of all this attention.

Am introduced to hundreds of people—quite as many men as women, which impresses me, and which I feel vaguely should go at least half-way towards solving American Woman Problem, if only I could make the connection —but clarity of thought distinctly impaired, probably by cocktails.

Attractive woman in blue tells me that she knows a friend of mine: Mrs. Tressider? I in-

stinctively reply. Yes, Mrs. Tressider. And The
Boy too. He doesn't look strong. I assert—
without the slightest justification—that he is
much stronger than he was, and begin to talk
about the Fair. Am told in return that I *must*
visit the Hall of Science, go up the Observation Tower, and inspect the Belgian Village.

Complete stranger tells me that I am dining
at her apartment to-morrow, another lady adds
that she is looking forward to seeing me on
Sunday at her home in the country, an elderly
gentleman remarks that he is so glad he is to
have the pleasure of giving me lunch and taking me round the Fair, and another complete,
and charming, stranger informs me that Arthur
and I are to have tea at her house when we
visit Chicago University.

Am beginning to feel slightly dazed—cocktails have undoubtedly contributed to this—
but gratified beyond description at so much attention and kindness, and have hazy idea of
writing letter home to explain that I am evidently of much greater importance than any of
us have ever realised.

Am brought slightly down to earth again by

remembrance that I am not in Chicago entirely for purpose of enjoyment, and that to-morrow Pete is escorting me to important department store, where I am to sign books and deliver short speech.

Decide that I must learn this by heart overnight, but am taken to a symphony concert, come back very late, and go to bed instead. *October 31st.*—Am called for in the morning by Pete—hat still at very dashing angle—and we walk through the streets. He tells me candidly that he does not like authors, I say that I don't either, and we get on extremely well.

Department store is the most impressive thing I have ever seen in my life and the largest. We inspect various departments, including Modern Furniture, which consists of a number of rooms containing perfectly square sofas, colored glass animals, cocktail-appliances, and steel chairs. Am a good deal impressed and think that it is all a great improvement on older style, but at the same time cannot possibly conceive of Robert reading *The Times* seated on oblong black-and-green divan with small, glass-topped table projecting from the wall beside him and statuette of naked angular woman with large elbows exactly opposite.

Moreover, no provision made anywhere for housing children, and do not like to enquire what, if anything, is ever done for them.

Admirable young gentleman who shows us round says that The Modern Kitchen will be of special interest to me, and ushers us into it. Pete, at this stage, looks slightly sardonic, and I perceive that he is as well aware as I am myself that The Modern Kitchen is completely wasted on me. Further reflection also occurs to me that if Pete were acquainted with Cook he would realise even better than he does why I feel that The Modern Kitchen is not destined to hold any significant place in my life.

Pete informs me that he is anxious to introduce me to charming and capable woman, friend of his, who runs the book department of the store. He tells me her name, and I immediately forget it again, although convinced that she is all he says. Later on, short exercise in Pelmanism enables me to connect wave in her hair with first name, which is Marcella. Remaining and more important half continues

[87]

elusive, and I therefore call her nothing. Am impressed by her office, which is entirely plastered with photographs, mostly inscribed, of celebrities. She asks if I know various of these. I have to reply each time that I don't, and begin to feel inferior. Become absent-minded, and hear myself, on being asked if I haven't met George Bernard Shaw, replying No, but I know who he is. This reply not a success, and Marcella ceases to probe into the state of my literary connections.

Soon afterwards I am escorted back to book department—should like to linger amongst First Editions, or even New Juveniles, but this is not encouraged—and young subordinate of Marcella's announces that quite a nice lot of people are waiting. Last week, she adds, they had Hervey Allen. Foresee exactly what she is going to say next, which is What do I think of *Anthony Adverse*, and pretend to be absorbed in small half-sheet of paper on which I have written rather illegible notes.

Quite a nice lot of people turns out to mean between four and five hundred ladies, with a sprinkling of men, all gathered round a little dais with a table, behind which I am told to take up my stand. Feel a great deal more inclined to crawl underneath it and stay there, but quite realise that this is, naturally, out of the question.

Marcella says a few words—I remind myself that nothing in the world can last for ever, and anyway they will none of them ever set eyes on me again after this afternoon—and plunge forthwith into speech.

Funny story goes well—put in another one which I have just thought of, and which isn't so good—but that goes well, too. Begin to think that I really am a speaker after all and wonder why nobody at home has ever said anything about it, and how I am ever to make them believe it without sounding conceited.

Sit down amidst applause and try to look modest until I suddenly catch sight of literary friend Arthur and his friend Billy, who have evidently been listening. Am rather agitated at this and feel that, instead of looking modest, I merely look foolish.

At this point Pete, who hasn't even pretended to listen to me, for which I am grateful rather than otherwise, reappears from some quite other department where he has sensibly been spending his time, and says that I had better autograph a few books, as People will Like It.

His idea of a few books runs into hundreds, and I sit and sign them and feel very important indeed. Streams of ladies walk past and we exchange a few words. Most of them ask How does one write a book? and several tell me that they heard something a few weeks ago which definitely *ought* to go into a book. This is usually a witticism perpetrated by a dear little grandchild, aged six last July, but is sometimes merely a Funny Story already known to me, and—probably—to everybody else in the civilised world. I say Thank you, Thank you very much, and continue to sign my name. Idle fancy crosses my mind that it would be fun if I was J. P. Morgan, and all this was cheques.

After a time Marcella retrieves me, and says very nicely that she has not forgotten I am an Englishwoman, and will want my Tea. Am not fond of tea at the best of times, and seldom take it, but cannot of course say so, and only refer to Arthur and his friend Billy, who may be waiting for me. No, not at all, says Marcella. They are buying tortoises. Tortoises? Yes, tiny little tortoises. There is, asserts Marcella, a display of them downstairs, with different flowers handpainted on their shells. She takes advantage of the stunned condition into which this plunges me to take me back to her office where we have tea—English note struck by the fact that it is pitch black, and we have lemon instead of milk—and Pete rejoins us, and confirms rumor as to floral tortoises being on sale, only he refers to them as turtles. Later on, am privileged to view them, and they crawl about in a little basin filled with water and broken shells, and display unnatural-looking bunches of roses and forget-me-nots on their backs.

Sign more books after tea, and am then taken away by friend Arthur, who says that his mother is waiting for me at the English-speaking Union. (Why not at home, which I should much prefer?) However, the English-speaking Union is very pleasant. I meet a number of people, they ask what I think of America, and if I am going to California, and I say in return that I look forward to visiting the Fair, and we part amicably.

Interesting and unexpected encounter with one lady, dressed in black and green, who says that when in New York she met my children's late French governess. I scream with excitement, and black-and-green lady looks rather pitying, and says Oh yes, the world is quite a small place. I say contentiously No, no, not as small as all that, and Mademoiselle and I met in New York, and I do so hope she is happy and with nice people. She is, replies black-and-green lady severely, with perfectly delightful people—Southerners—one of our very oldest Southern families. They all speak with a real Southern accent. Stop myself just in time from saying that Mademoiselle will probably correct that, and ask instead if the children are fond of her. Black-and-green lady only repeats, in reply, that her friends belong to the oldest Southern family in the South, practically, and moves off looking as though she rather disapproves of me.

This encounter, for reason which I cannot identify, has rather thrown me off my balance, and I shortly afterwards ask Arthur if we cannot go home. He says Yes, in the most amiable way and takes me away in a taxi, with his very pretty sister. Enquire of her where and how I can possibly get my hair washed, and she at once undertakes to make all necessary arrangements, and says that the place that does *her* hair can very well do mine. (As she is a particularly charming blonde, at least ten years younger than I am, the results will probably be entirely different, but keep this pessimistic reflection to myself.)

Literary friend Arthur, with great good feeling, says that he knows there are some letters waiting for me, which I shall wish to read in peace, and that he is sure I should like to rest before dinner-party, to which he is taking me at eight o'clock. (Should like to refer Katherine Ellen Blatt to dear Arthur, for lessons in *savoir-faire*.)

Letters await me in my room, but exercise great self-control by tearing off my hat, throwing my coat on the floor, and dashing gloves and bag into different corners of the room before I sit down to read them.

Only one is from England: Our Vicar's Wife writes passionate enquiry as to whether I am going anywhere near Arizona, as boy in whom she and Our Vicar took great interest in their *first* parish—north London, five-and-twenty years ago—is supposed to have gone there and done very well. Will I make enquiries—name was Sydney Cripps, and has one front tooth missing, knocked out at cricket—has written to Our Vicar from time to time, but last occasion nearly twelve years ago—Time, adds Our Vicar's Wife, passes. All is well at home—very strange not to see me about—Women's Institute Committee met last week, how difficult it is to please everybody.

Can believe from experience that this is, indeed, so.

November 1st.—Visit the World's Fair in company with Arthur and his family. Buildings all very modern and austere, except for coloring, which is inclined to be violent, but aspect as a whole is effective and impressive, and much to be preferred to customary imitations of ancient Greece. Individual exhibits admirably displayed, and total area of space covered must be enormous, whether lake—of which I see large bits here and there—is included or not. Private cars not admitted—which I think sensible—but rickshaws available, drawn by University students—to whom, everybody says, It's Interesting to Talk—and small motor-buses go quietly round and round the Fair.

Arthur and I patronise rickshaws—I take a good look at my University Student, and decide that conversation would probably benefit neither of us—and visit various buildings. Hall of Science not amongst our successes, unfortunately, as the sight of whole skeletons, portions of the human frame executed in plaster, and realistic maps of sinews and blood-vessels, all ranged against the wall in glass show-cases, merely causes me to hurry past with my eyes shut. Arthur is sympathetic, and tells me that there *is* an exhibit of Live Babies in Incubators to be seen, but cannot decide whether he means that this would be better than scientific wonders at present surrounding us, or worse.

Resume rickshaws, and visit Jade Chinese Temple, which is lovely, Prehistoric Animals— unpleasant impression of primitive man's existence derived from these, but should like to have seen a brontosaurus in the flesh nevertheless— and Belgian Village, said to be replica of fifteenth century. (If not fifteenth, then sixteenth. Cannot be sure.)

Here Arthur and I descend, and walk up and down stone steps and cobbled streets, and watch incredibly clean-looking peasants in picturesque costumes dancing hand in hand and every now and then stamping. Have always hitherto associated this with Russians, but evidently wrong.

Just as old Flemish Clock on old Flemish Town Hall clangs out old Flemish Air, and Arthur and I tell one another that this is beautifully done, rather brassy voice from concealed loudspeaker is inspired to enquire: O boy! What about that new tooth paste? Old Flemish atmosphere goes completely to bits, and Arthur and I, in disgust, retire to Club, where we meet his family, and have most excellent lunch.

Everyone asks what I want to see next, and Arthur's mother says that she has a few friends coming to dinner, but is thrown into consternation by Arthur's father, who says that he has

Arthur and I patronize rickshaws

invited two South Americans to come in afterwards. Everyone says South Americans? as if they were pterodactyls at the very least, and antecedents are enquired into, but nothing whatever transpires except that they are South Americans and that nobody knows anything about them, not even their names.

Return to Fair after lunch—new rickshaw student, less forbidding-looking than the last, and I say feebly that It is very hot for November, and he replies that he can tell by my accent that I come from England and he supposes it's always foggy there, and I say No not always, and nothing further passes between us. Am evidently not gifted, where interesting students from American Colleges are concerned, and decide to do nothing more in this line. More exhibits follow—mostly very good—and Arthur says that he thinks we ought to see the North American Indians.

He accordingly pays large sum of money which admits us into special enclosures where authentic Red Indians are stamping about— (stamping definitely discredited henceforward as a Russian monopoly)—and uttering sounds exclusively on two notes, all of which, so far as I can tell, consist of Wah Wah! and nothing else. Listen to this for nearly forty minutes but am not enthusiastic. Neither is Arthur, and we shortly afterwards go home.

Write postcards to Rose, the children, and Robert, and after some thought send one to Cook, although entirely uncertain as to whether this will gratify her or not. Am surprised, and rather disturbed, to find that wording of Cook's postcard takes more thought than that on all the others put together.

Small dinner takes place later on, and consists of about sixteen people, including a lady whose novel won the Pulitzer prize, a lady who writes poetry—very, very well-known, though not, unhappily, to me—a young gentleman who has something to do with Films, an older one who is connected with Museums, and delightful woman in green, who says that she knows Devonshire and has stayed with the Frobishers. Did she, I rashly enquire, enjoy it? Well, she replies tolerantly, Devonshire is a lovely part of the world, but she is afraid Sir William Frobisher dislikes Americans. I protest, and she then adds, conclusively, that Sir W. told her *himself* how much he disliked Americans. Feel that it would indeed be idle to try and get round this, so begin to talk at once about the Fair.

Dinner marvellous, as usual—company very agreeable—and my neighbor—Museums—offers to conduct me to see Chicago Historical Museum at ten o'clock next morning.

Just as dinner is over, two extremely elegant young gentlemen, with waists and superbly smooth *coiffures*, come in and bow gracefully to our hostess. New York friend, Billy, hisses at me: "The South Americans" and I nod assent, and wonder how on earth they are going to be introduced, when nobody knows their names. This, however, is achieved by hostess who simply asks them what they are called, and then introduces everybody else.

Am told afterwards that neither of them speaks much English, and that Arthur's father asked them questions all the evening. No one tells me whether they answered them or not, and I remain mildly curious on the point.

November 4th.—Singular and interesting op-

[99]

portunity is offered me to contrast Sunday spent on Long Island and Sunday spent in equivalent country district outside Chicago, called Lake Forest, where I am invited to lunch and spend the afternoon. Enquire of Arthur quite early if this is to be a large party. He supposes About Thirty. Decide at once to put on the Coming Molyneux's best effort—white daisies on blue silk. But, says Arthur, country clothes. Decide to substitute wool coat and skirt, with red beret. And, says Arthur, he is taking me on to dinner with very, very rich acquaintance, also at Lake Forest. I revert, mentally, to blue silk and daisies, and say that I suppose it won't matter if we're not in evening dress? Oh, replies Arthur, we've got to take evening clothes with us, and change there. Our hostess won't hear of anything else. I take a violent dislike to her on the spot, and say that I'm not sure I want to go at all. At this Arthur is gloomy, but firm. *He* doesn't want to go, either, and neither does Billy, but we can't get out of it now. We must simply pack our evening clothes in bags and *go*. Have not sufficient moral courage to rebel any further, and instead

[100]

consider the question of packing up my evening clothes. Suit-case is too large, and attaché-case too small, but finally decide on the latter, which will probably mean ruin to evening frock.

November 5th.—Literary friend Arthur, still plunged in gloom, takes Billy and me by car to Lake Forest, about thirty miles from Chicago. We talk about grandmothers—do not know why or how this comes to pass—and then about Scotland. Scenery very beautiful, but climate bad. Arthur once went to Holyrood, but saw no bloodstains. Billy has a relation who married the owner of a Castle in Ross-shire and they live there and have pipers every evening. I counter this by saying that I have a friend, married to a distinguished historian or something, at Edinburgh University. Wish I hadn't said "or something" as this casts an air of spuriousness over the whole story. Try to improve on it by adding firmly that they live in Wardic Avenue, Edinburgh—but this is received in silence.

(*Query:* Why are facts invariably received so much less sympathetically than fictions?

Had I only said that distinguished historian and his wife lived in a cellar of Edinburgh Castle and sold Edinburgh rock, reactions of Arthur and Billy probably much more enthusiastic.)

Arrive at about one o'clock. House, explains Arthur, belongs to great friends of his—charming people—Mrs. F. writes novels—sister won Pulitzer prize with another novel. At this I interject Yes, Yes, I met her the other day—and feel like a dear old friend of the family.

House, says Arthur all over again—at which I perceive that I must have interrupted him before he'd finished, and suddenly remember that Robert has occasionally complained of this —House belongs to Mr. and Mrs. F. and has been left entirely unaltered since it was first built in 1874, furniture and all. It is, in fact, practically a Museum Piece.

Discover this to be indeed no over-statement, and am enchanted with house, which is completely Victorian, and has fretwood brackets in every available corner, and a great deal of furniture. Am kindly welcomed, and taken upstairs to leave my coat and take off my hat.

Spend the time instead in looking at gilt clock under glass shade, wool-and-bead mats, and colored pictures of little girls in pinafores playing with large white kittens. Have to be retrieved by hostess's daughter, who explains that she thought I might have lost my way. I apologise and hope that I'm not late for lunch.

This fear turns out later to be entirely groundless, as luncheon-party—about thirty-five people—assembles by degrees on porch, and drinks cocktails, and nobody sits down to lunch until three o'clock. Have pleasant neighbors on either side, and slightly tiresome one opposite, who insists on talking across the table and telling me that I must go to the South, whatever I do. She herself comes of a Southern family, and has never lost her Southern accent, as I have no doubt noticed. Am aware that she intends me to assent to this, but do not do so, and conversation turns to *Anthony Adverse* as usual—and the popularity of ice-cream in America. Lunch over at about four o'clock— can understand why tea, as a meal, does not exist in the U.S.A.—and we return to the porch, and everyone says that this is the Indian Summer.

Find myself sitting with elderly man, who civilly remarks that he wants to hear about the book I have written. Am aware that this cannot possibly be true, but take it in the spirit in which it is meant, and discuss instead the British Museum—which he knows much better than I do—trout-fishing—about which neither of us knows anything whatever—and the state of the dollar.

Soon afterwards Arthur, with fearful recrudescence of despair, tells me that there is nothing for it, as we've got another forty miles to drive, but to say good-bye and go. We may not *want* to, but we simply haven't any choice, he says.

After this we linger for about thirty-five minutes longer, repeating how sorry we are that we've got to go, and hearing how very sorry everybody else is as well. Eventually find ourselves in car again, suit-cases with evening clothes occupying quite a lot of space, and again causing Arthur to lament pertinacity of hostess who declined to receive us in ordinary day clothes.

Fog comes on—is this a peculiarity of Indian Summer?—chauffeur takes two or three wrong turnings, but says that he knows where we shall Come Out—and Billy goes quietly to sleep. Arthur and I talk in subdued voices for several minutes, but get louder and louder as we become more interested, and Billy wakes up and denies that he has ever closed an eye at all.

Silence then descends upon us all, and I lapse into thoughts of Robert, the children, and immense width and depth of the Atlantic Ocean. Have, as usual, killed and buried us all, myself included, several times over before we arrive.

Just as we get out of car—Billy falls over one of the suit-cases, and says Damn—Arthur mutters that I *must* remember to look at the pictures. Wonderful collection, and hostess likes them to be admired. This throws me off my balance completely, and I follow very superb and monumental butler with my eyes fixed on every picture I see, in series of immense rooms through which we are led. Result of this is that I practically collide with hostess, advancing gracefully to receive us, and that my rejoinders to her cries of welcome are totally lacking in *empressement*, as I am still wondering how soon I ought to say anything about the pictures, and what means I can adopt to sound as if I really knew something about them. Hostess recalls me to myself by enquiring passionately if we have brought evening things, as she has rooms all ready for us to change in.

Am struck by this preoccupation with evening clothes, and interesting little speculation presents itself as to whether she suffers from obsession on the point, and if so could psychoanalysis be of any help? Treatment undoubtedly very expensive, but need not, in this case, be considered.

Just as I have mentally consigned her to luxurious nursing-home, with two specialists and a trained nurse, hostess again refers to our evening clothes, and says that we had better come up and see the rooms in which we are to dress. Follow her upstairs—more pictures all the way up, and in corridor of vast length— I hear Arthur referring to "that marvellous

Toulouse-Lautrec" and look madly about, but cannot guess which one he means, as all alike look to me marvellous, except occasional still-life which I always detest—and shortly afterwards I am parted from Arthur and Billy, and shown into complete *suite*, with bedroom, bathroom, and sitting-room. Hostess says solicitously: Can I manage?

Yes, on the whole I think I can.

(Wonder what she would feel about extremely shabby bedroom at home, total absence of either private bathroom or Toulouse-Lautrec, and sitting-room downstairs in which Robert, children, cat, dog, and myself all congregate together round indifferent wood-fire. This vision, however, once more conducive to homesickness, and hastily put it aside and look at all the books in the five bookcases to see what I can read in the bath.)

Am surprised and gratified to find that I have remembered to pack everything I want, and perform satisfactory *toilette*, twice interrupted by offers of assistance from ladies' maid, who looks astonished when I refuse them. Look at myself in three different mirrors, decide—

rather ungenerously—that I am better-looking
than my hostess, and on this reassuring reflection, proceed downstairs.

November 5th (continued).—Decide that I
am, beyond a doubt, making acquaintance with
Millionaire Life in America, and that I must
take mental notes of everything I see and eat,
for benefit of Robert and the Women's Institute. Hostess, waiting in the drawing-room, has
now gone into mauve chiffon, triple necklace of
large uncut amethysts, and at least sixteen
amethyst bracelets. Am definitely envious of
uncut amethysts, and think to myself that they
would look well on me.

Hostess is vivacious—talks to me in a
sparkling manner about World's Fair, the South
—which I must, at all costs, visit—and California which is, she says, overrated. But not,
I urge, the climate? Oh yes, the climate too.
Am disillusioned by this, and think of saying
that even Wealth cannot purchase Ideal Cli-
matic Conditions, but this far too reminiscent
of *The Fairchild Family*, and is instantly
dismissed.

Arthur and Billy come down, and I experience renewed tendency to cling to their society in the midst of so much that is unfamiliar, and reflect that I shall never again blame dear Robin for invariably electing to sit next to his own relations at parties. Guests arrive—agreeable man with bald head comes and talks to me, and says that he has been looking forward to meeting me again, and I try, I hope successfully, to conceal fact that I had no idea that we had ever met before.

Dinner follows—table is made of looking-glass, floor has looking-glass let into it and so has ceiling. This arrangement impressive in the extreme, though no doubt more agreeable to some of us than to others. Try to imagine Robert, Our Vicar, and even old Mrs. Blenkinsop in these surroundings, and fail completely.

After dinner retire to quite another drawing-room, and sit next yellow-satin lady with iron-grey hair, who cross-questions me rather severely on my impressions of America, and tells me that I don't really like Chicago, as English people never do, but that I shall adore Boston. Am just preparing to contradict her when she spills her coffee all over me. We all scream, and I get to my feet, dripping coffee over no-doubt-invaluable Persian rug, and iron-grey lady, with more presence of mind than regard for truth, exclaims that I must have done it with my elbow and what a pity it is! Cannot, in the stress of the moment, think of any form of words combining both perfect candor and absolute courtesy, in which to tell her that she is not speaking the truth and that her own clumsiness is entirely responsible for disaster. Iron-grey woman takes the initiative and calls for cold water—hot water no good at all, the colder the better, for coffee.

(*Query:* Why does she know so much about it? Is it an old habit of hers to spill coffee? Probably.)

Extensive sponging follows, and everybody except myself says that It ought to be All Right now—which I know very well only means that they are all thoroughly tired of the subject and wish to stop talking about it.

Sit down again at furthest possible distance from iron-grey woman—who is now informing us that if my frock had been velvet she would have advised steaming, *not* sponging—and

[110]

realise that, besides having ruined my frock, I am also running grave risk of rheumatic fever, owing to general dampness.

Remainder of the evening, so far as I am concerned, lacks *entrain*.

November 6th.—Chicago visit draws to a close, and Pete, after a last solemn warning to me about the importance of visiting bookstores in all the towns I go to, returns to New York, but tells me that we shall meet again somewhere or other very soon. Hope that this is meant as a pleasant augury, rather than a threat, but am by no means certain.

November 7th.—Wake up in the middle of the night and remember that I never asked Robert to water indoor bulbs, planted by me in September and left, as usual, in attic. Decide to send him a cable in the morning. Doze again, but wake once more with strong conviction that cable would not be a success as (a) It might give Robert a shock, (b) He would think it extravagant. Decide to write letter about bulbs instead.

Final spate of social activities marks the day, and includes further visit to World's Fair, when I talk a great deal about buying presents for everybody at home, but in the long run only buy Indian silver bracelet with turquoise, for Caroline C. (Will take up no extra room in flat, and am hoping she will wear it, rather than leave it about.)

Telegram is brought me in the course of the afternoon, am seized by insane conviction that it must be from Robert to say he *has* watered the bulbs, but this stretching long arm of co-incidence altogether too far, and decide instead that Robin has been mortally injured at football. Turns out to be communication of enormous length inviting me to lecture in New York some weeks hence followed by tea at which many distinguished writers hope to be present which will mean many important contacts also publicity Stop Very cordially Katherine Ellen Blatt. Read all this through at least four times before any of it really sinks in, and then send back brief, but I hope civil, refusal.

Eat final dinner with Arthur and his family —tell them how much I hope they will all come and stay with Robert and myself next summer —and part from them with extreme regret.

Just as I am leaving, another telegram arrives: Please reconsider decision cannot take no for an answer literary tea really important function will receive wide press publicity letter follows Stop Very sincerely Katherine Ellen Blatt.

Am a good deal stunned by this and decide to wait a little before answering.

Arthur sees me off at station, and I board immense train on which I appear to be the only passenger. Procedure ensues with which I am rapidly becoming familiar, including unsatisfactory wash in small Toilet Compartment which only provides revolting little machine that oozes powder, instead of decent soap. Reflect how much Robert would dislike this. Thought of Robert is, as usual, too much for me and I retire to sleeping accommodation behind customary green curtains, and prepare to sink into a sentimental reverie, but discover that I am sitting on green paper bag into which porter has put my hat. Revulsion of feeling follows, and I give way to anger instead of sorrow.

November 8th.—Consider in some detail American preference for travelling at night, and decide that I do not, on the whole, share it. Meals undoubtedly excellent, but other arrangements poor, and arrival in small hours of the morning utterly uncongenial.

Cleveland reached at 8 A.M.—eyes still bunged with sleep and spirits at a very low ebb—and am met by extremely blue-eyed Miss V. from Bookstore who says that she has Heard About me from Pete. She gets into a car with me but does not say where she is taking me, and talks instead about Winchester, American novels, and the Chicago World's Fair. (Can foresee that long before the end of tour I shall have said all I have to say about World's Fair, and shall find myself trying to invent brand-new details.)

Drive through a great many streets, and past large numbers of superb shop-fronts, and presently Miss V. says in a reverent voice, *There* is Halle Brothers, and I say Where, and have a vague idea that she is referring to local Siamese Twins, but this turns out complete mistake and Halle Brothers revealed as enormous, really splendid-looking department store, in which Miss V. is in charge of book department. Moreover Mrs. Halle, it now appears, is to be my hostess in Cleveland and we have now practically reached her house.

At this I look frantically in my hand-bag, discover that I have left lip-stick in the train, do what I can with powder-compact but results on pale-green complexion not at all satisfactory, and realise, not for the first time, that accidental sitting on my hat in the train did it no good.

Mrs. Halle, however, receives me kindly in spite of these misfortunes, shows me very nice bedroom which she says belongs to her daughter Katherine, now in Europe, and says that breakfast will be ready when I am. Spend some time walking round Katherine's bedroom, and am deeply impressed by her collection of books, which comprises practically everything that I have always meant to read. Decide that Katherine must be wholly given over to learning, but reverse this opinion on going into Katherine's bathroom and finding it filled with colored glass bottles, pots, and jars of the

[115]

most exotic description. Evidently other and
more frivolous pre-occupations as well.

This conjecture confirmed when I meet Katherine's sister Jane at breakfast—very pretty
and well-dressed, and can probably do everything in the world well. Distinct tendency
comes over me to fall into rather melancholy
retrospect concerning my own youth, utterly
denuded of any of the opportunities afforded
to present generation. Remind myself in time,
however, that this reflection is as wholly unoriginal as any in the world, and that I myself
invariably dislike and despise those who give
vent to it.

Excellent coffee and bacon help further to
restore me, and I decide that almost every
sorrow can probably be assuaged by a respectable meal. (Mem: Try to remember this and
act upon it next time life appears to be wholly
intolerable.)

Programme for the day is then unfolded,
and comprises—to my surprise—inspection of
three schools. The blue-eyed Miss V. has said
that I am interested in education. Think this
over, decide that I ought to be interested in

education, and that therefore I probably am, and accept with what is invariably referred to by dear Vicky as alacricity.

Morning is accordingly spent in visiting schools, of which I like two and am staggered by the third, which is said to be on totally New Age lines, and designed in order to enable the very young—ages two to nine—to develop their own life-pattern without interference.

The head mistress says that the Little Ones are never interfered with, and that punishments are unknown. Even supervision is made as unobtrusive as possible. This she demonstrates by conducting us to landing on the staircase, where large window overlooks playground. Here, she says, teachers and parents can watch the little people at play. Play very often a great revelation of character.

Can see no reason in the world why little people should not look up from play and plainly perceive the noses of their parents and guardians earnestly pressed to the window above them—but do not, naturally, say so.

We then inspect Art—angular drawings of crooked houses and deformed people and animals, painted in pale splotches of red and green and yellow—Handiwork—paper boxes with defective corners, and blue paper mats—and Carpentry—a great many pieces of wood and some sawdust.

Just as we leave Bathrooms—each child, says our guide passionately, has its own little toothbrush in its own little mug—on our way downstairs to Gymnasium, Miss V. draws my attention to a door with a little grille in it, through which we both peer in some astonishment.

Infant child aged about three is revealed, sitting in solitude on tiny little chair in front of tiny little table gazing thoughtfully at a dinner-plate. What, I ask, is this? She looks distressed and replies Oh, that's The Food-Problem.

We all three contemplate this distressing enigma in silence, and the Food-Problem gazes back at us with intelligent interest and evident gratification, and we shortly afterwards retire.

Should be very sorry indeed to see New Age methods adopted at eminently sane and

Each child, says our guide passionately, has its own little toothbrush in its own little mug

straightforward establishment where Vicky is—
I hope—at present receiving education.

November 9th.—Life in Cleveland agreeable,
but rushed. Bookstore talk takes place as
ordained by Pete, and is principally remarkable because Lowell Thomas, celebrated American writer, precedes me and gives very amusing lecture. Entire book department turned
upside-down searching for green ink, as it is,
says Miss V., well-known that Lowell T. never
will autograph his books in any other colour.
Am frightfully impressed by this, and join in
green-ink hunt. It is finally run to earth, and
I suggest gumming on small label with L.T.'s
name and telling him that it has been waiting
ever since his last visit. Am unfortunately never
informed whether this ingenious, though perhaps not very straightforward scheme, is actually adopted.

Shake hands with Lowell Thomas afterwards, and like the look of him, and buy two
of his books, which are all about Arabia, and
will do for Robert. He autographs them in
green ink, and I seriously contemplate telling
Miss V. that it will be utterly impossible for

[119]

me to sign a single volume of my own unless
I can do so with an old-fashioned goose-quill
and blue blotting-paper.

Rather amusing incident then ensues, on my
proffering modest request that I may be allowed to Wash My Hands. Will I, says Miss
V. anxiously, be *very careful indeed*? No later
than last year, celebrated Winner of Pulitzer
Prize succeeded in locking the door in such a
way that it was totally impossible to unlock
it again, and there she was, says Miss V. agi-
tatedly, unable to make anybody hear, and
meanwhile everybody was looking for her all
over the store, and couldn't imagine what had
happened, and eventually A Man had to break
down the door.

Am horrified by this tragedy, and promise to
exercise every care, but feel that Miss V. is
still reluctant to let me embark on so perilous
an enterprise. Moreover am stopped no less
than three times, on my way down small and
obscure passage, and told by various young
employees to be very careful indeed, last year
Pulitzer Prize-winner was locked in there for
hours and hours and couldn't be got out, man

had to be sent for, door eventually broken down. Am reminded of the Mistletoe Bough and wonder if this distressing modern version has ever been immortalized in literature, and if not how it could be done.

Various minor inspirations flit across my mind, but must be dealt with later, and I concentrate on warnings received, and succeed in locking and unlocking door with complete success.

Pulitzer Prize-winner either remarkably unfortunate, or else strangely deficient in elementary manual dexterity. Am taken home in car by Mrs. Halle—who tells me on the way the whole story of Pulitzer Prize-winner and her misfortune all over again—and am tactfully invited to rest before dinner.

(Rumor that American hostesses give one no time to breathe definitely unjust.)

November 10th.—Bid reluctant farewell to Cleveland. Last day is spent in visiting bookstore, signing name—which I shall soon be able to do in my sleep—and being taken by the Halle family to see film: "Private Life of Henry VIII." Charles Laughton is, as usual, marvellous, but film itself seems to me over-rated. Tell Mrs. H. that I would leave home any day for C. Laughton, at which she looks surprised, and I feel bound to add that I don't really mean it literally. She then takes me to the station and we part amicably with mutual hopes of again meeting, in England or else-where.

Just as I am preparing to board train, Miss V. arrives with English mail for me, which she has received at eleventh hour and is kindly determined that I shall have without delay. Am extremely grateful, and settle down to un-wonted luxury of immediate and uninterrupted reading.

Robert, Vicky and Robin all well, Robert much occupied with British Legion concert which he says was well attended, but accom-panist suddenly overcome by influenza and great difficulty in finding a substitute. Miss Pankhurst played Violin Solo and this, says Robert, was much too long. Can well believe it. Nothing whatever in garden, but one indoor bulb shows signs of life. Am not at all exhila-rated at this, and feel sure that bulbs would have done better under my own eye. Early Romans should certainly be well above ground by now.

Only remaining news is that Lady B. has offered to organise Historical Pageant in the village next summer, featuring herself as Mary Queen of Scots, and everybody else as morris-dancers, jesters, knights and peasantry. Robert and Our Vicar dead against this, and Our Vicar's Wife said to have threatened to resign the living. Living not hers to resign, actually, but am in complete sympathy with general attitude implied, and think seriously of cabling to say so.

In any case, Why Mary Queen of Scots? No possible connection with remote village in Devonshire. Can only suppose that Lady B. can think of no better way of displaying her pearls.

Surprised to find that dear Rose has actually remembered my existence—no doubt helped by extraordinarily interesting series of postcards sent at intervals ever since I left—and has written short letter to say that she hopes I am having a very interesting time, and she envies me for being in America, London is very cold and foggy. Brief references follow to concert, lecture on child-guidance, and several new plays recently attended by Rose, and she closes with best love and is mine ever. P.S. Agatha is engaged to Betty's brother, followed by three marks of exclamation.

Have never, to my certain knowledge, heard of Agatha, Betty, or the brother in my life.

Large envelope addressed by Caroline Concannon comes next, and discloses number of smaller envelopes, all evidently containing bills, also card of invitation to a Public Dinner, price one guinea, postcard from Cissie Crabbe—saying that it is a Long While since she had news of me—and a letter from C.C. herself.

This proves to be agreeably scandalous, and relates astonishing behavior of various prominent people. C.C. also adds that she thinks it will amuse me to hear that a great friend of hers is divorcing his wife and twelve co-respondents will be cited, there could have been many more, but only twelve names have come out. Am disturbed by Caroline's idea of what is likely to amuse me, but after awhile feel that perhaps she has not wholly misjudged me after all.

Forgive her everything when final page of letter reveals that she has been to visit both Robin and Vicky at school, and gives full and satisfactory account of each, even entering into details regarding Robin's purchases at penny-in-the-slot machines on pier, and Vicky's plate.

Letter concludes, as usual, with sweeping and optimistic assertion that Everything in Doughty Street is Absolutely All Right, the carpets want cleaning rather badly, and Caroline will try and get them done before I get back, also the chandelier, absolutely pitch-black.

Caroline Concannon is followed by Felicity —blue envelope and rather spidery handwriting—who hopes that I am making some money. She herself is overdrawn at the Bank and can't make it out, she *knows* she has spent far less than usual in the last six months, but it's always the way. Felicity further hopes that I have good news of the children, and it will be nice to know I'm safely home again, and ends with renewed reference to finance, which is evi-

dently an overwhelming pre-occupation. Feel
sorry for Felicity, and decide to send her another postcard, this time from Toronto.

Remaining correspondence includes earnest
letter of explanation—now some weeks out-of-
date—from laundry, concerning pair of Boy's
Pants—about which I remember nothing whatever—begging letter from a Society which says
that it was established while King William IV
was still on the throne—and completely illegible letter from Mary Kellway.

Make really earnest effort to decipher this,
as dear Mary always so amusing and original—
but can make out nothing whatever beyond my
own name—which I naturally know already—
and statement that Mary's husband has been
busy with what looks like—but of course cannot be—pencils and geranium-tops—and that
the three children have gone either to bed, to
the bad, to board, or to live at place which
might be either Brighton, Ilford, or Egypt.

Feel that this had better be kept until time
permits of my deciphering it, and that all comment should be reserved until I can feel really
convinced of exact nature of items enumerated.

In the meanwhile, dear Mary has received no postcards at all, and decide that this omission must be repaired at earliest opportunity.

November 11th.—Reach Toronto at preposterous hour of 5.55 A.M. and decide against night-travelling once and for ever, day having actually started with Customs inspection considerably before dawn. Decide to try and see what I can of Canada and glue my face to the window, but nothing visible for a long while. Am finally rewarded by superb sun-rise, but eyelids feel curiously stiff and intelligence at lowest possible ebb. Involve myself in rather profound train of thought regarding dependence of artistic perception upon physical conditions, but discover in the midst of it that I am having a nightmare about the children both being drowned, and have dropped two books and one glove.

Colored porter appears with clothes-brush, and is evidently convinced that I cannot possibly present myself to Canadian inspection without previously submitting to his ministrations. As I feel that he is probably right, I stand up and am rather half-heartedly dealt with, and

[127]

then immediately sit down again, no doubt in original collection of dust, and weakly present porter with ten cents, at which he merely looks disgusted and says nothing.

Train stops, and I get out of it, and find myself—as so often before—surrounded by luggage on strange and ice-cold platform, only too well aware that I probably look even more *dégommée* than I feel.

Canadian host and hostess, with great good feeling, have both turned out to meet me, and am much impressed at seeing that neither cold nor early rising have impaired complexion of my hostess. Find myself muttering quotation:

"Alike to her were time and tide,
November's snow and July's pride."

but Canadian host, Mr. Lee, says Did I speak? and I have to say No, no, nothing at all, and remind myself that talking aloud to oneself is well-known preliminary to complete mental breakdown. Make really desperate effort, decide that I *am* awake and that the day has begun—began, in fact, several hours ago—and that if only I am given a cup of very strong

[128]

coffee quite soon, I shall very likely find myself restored to normal degree of alertness.

Mr. Lee looks kind, Mrs. Lee—evidently several years younger—is cheerful and good-looking, and leads the way to small car waiting outside station.

This appears to me to be completely filled already by elderly lady in black, large dog, and little girl with pig-tails. These, I am told, are the near neighbors of the Lees. Should like to ask why this compels them to turn out at four o'clock in the morning in order to meet complete stranger, but do not, naturally, do so.

Explanation is presently proffered, to the effect that the Niagara Falls are only eighty miles away, and I am to visit them at once, and the little girl—Minnie—has never seen them either, so it seemed a good opportunity. Minnie, at this, jumps up and down the seat and has to be told to Hush, dear. Her mother adds that Minnie is very highly-strung. She always has been, and her mother is afraid she always will be. The doctor has said that she has, at nine years old, the brain of a child of fifteen. I look at Minnie, who at once assumes an interesting expression and puts her head on one side, at which I immediately look away again, and feel that I am not going to like Minnie. (This impression definitely gains ground as day goes on.) Mrs. Lee, on the other hand, earns gratitude almost amounting to affection by saying that I must have breakfast and a bath before anything else, and that both these objectives can be obtained on the way to Niagara.

I ask what about my luggage? and am told that a friend of some cousins living near Hamilton has arranged to call for it later and convey it to Mr. Lee's house. Am impressed, and decide that mutual readiness to oblige must be a feature of Canadian life. Make mental note to develop this theme when talking to Women's Institute at home.

At this point Minnie's mother suddenly asks What we are all here for, if not to help one another, and adds that for her part, her motto has always been: Lend a Hand. Revulsion of feeling at once overtakes me, and I abandon all idea of impressing the Women's Institute with the desirability of mutual good will.

Car takes us at great speed along admirable

roads—very tight squeeze on back seat, and Minnie kicks me twice on the shins and puts her elbow into my face once—and we reach house standing amongst trees.

Is this, I civilly enquire of Mrs. Lee, her home? Oh dear no. The Lees live right on the other side of Toronto. This is Dr. MacAfie's place, where we are all having breakfast. And a bath, adds Mrs. L., looking at me compassionately. Dr. MacAfie and his wife both turn out to be Scotch. They receive us kindly, and Mrs. L. at once advocates the bathroom for me.

Bath is a success, and I come down very hungry, convinced that it must be nearer lunchtime than breakfast-time. Clock, however, declares it to be just half-past seven. Find myself counting up number of hours that must elapse before I can hope to find myself in bed and asleep. Results of this calculation very discouraging.

Breakfast, which is excellent, restores me, and we talk about America—the States very unlike Canada—the Dominions—life in Canada very like life in the Old Country—snow very early this year—and my impressions of Chicago World's Fair.

Minnie interrupts a good deal, and says Need she eat bacon, and If she went on a big ship to England she knows she'd be very sick. At this everybody laughs—mine very perfunctory indeed—and her mother says that really, the things that child says, . . . and it's always been like that, ever since she was a tiny tot. Anecdotes of Minnie's infant witticisms follow, and I inwardly think of all the much more brilliant remarks made by Robin and Vicky. Should much like an opportunity for retailing these, and do my best to find one, but Minnie's mother gives me no opening whatever.

Expedition to Niagara ensues, and I am told on the way that it is important for me to see the Falls from the *Canadian* side, as this is greatly superior to the *American* side. Can understand this, in a way, as representing viewpoint of my present hosts, but hope that inhabitants of Buffalo, where I go next, will not prove equally patriotic and again conduct me immense distances to view phenomenon all over again.

[132]

Am, however, greatly impressed by Falls, and say so freely. Mr. Lee tells me that I really ought to see them by night, when lit up by electricity, and Mrs. Lee says No, that vulgarises them completely, and I reply Yes to both of them, and Minnie's mother asks What Minnie thinks of Niagara, to which Minnie squeaks out that she wants her dinner right away this minute, and we accordingly proceed to the Hotel.

Buy a great many postcards. Minnie watches this transaction closely, and says that she collects postcards. At this I very weakly present her with one of mine, and her mother says that I am really much too kind—with which I inwardly agree. This opinion intensified on return journey, when Minnie decides to sit on my lap, and asks me long series of complicated questions, such as Would I rather be an alligator who didn't eat people, or a man who had to make his living by stealing, or a tiny little midget in a circus? Reply to these and similar conundrums more or less in my sleep, and dimly hear Minnie's mother telling me that Minnie looks upon her as being just a great, big, elder sister, and always tells her everything just as it pops into her little head, and don't I feel that it's most important to have the complete confidence of one's children?

Can only think, at the moment, that it's most important to have a proper amount of sleep.

Mr. Lee's house is eventually attained, and proves to be outside Toronto. Minnie and her parent are dropped at their own door, and say that they will be popping in quite soon, and I get out of car and discover that I am alarmingly stiff, very cold, and utterly exhausted.

Am obliged to confess this state of affairs to Mrs. Lee, who is very kind, and advises bed. Can only apologise, and do as she suggests.

November 12th.—Spend comparatively quiet day, and feel better. Host and hostess agree that I must remain indoors, and as it snows violently I thankfully do so, and write very much over-due letters.

Quiet afternoon and evening of conversation. Mr. Lee wants to know about the Royal Family—of which, unfortunately, I can tell him little except what he can read for himself in the papers—and Mrs. Lee asks if I play much Bridge. She doesn't, she adds hastily,

Minnie's mother asks What Minnie thinks of Niagara

mean on Sundays. Am obliged to reply that I play very little on any day of the week, but try to improve this answer by adding that my husband is very good at cards. Then, says Mrs. Lee, do I garden? No—unfortunately not. Mrs. Lee seems disappointed, but supposes indulgently that writing a book takes up quite a lot of time, and I admit that it does, and we leave it at that.

Am rather disposed, after this effort, to sit and ponder on extreme difficulty of ever achieving continuity of conversation when in the society of complete strangers. Idle fancy crosses my mind that Mr. Alexander Woollcott would make nothing of it at all, and probably conduct whole conversation all by himself with complete success. Wonder—still more idly—if I shall send him a postcard about it, and whether he would like one of Niagara.

November 12th (*continued*).—Main purpose of Canadian visit—which is small lecture— safely accomplished. Audience kind, rather than enthusiastic. Mrs. Lee says that she could tell I was nervous. Cannot imagine more thoroughly discouraging comment than this.

Mr. Lee very kindly takes me to visit tallest building in the British Empire, which turns out to be a Bank. We inspect Board-rooms, offices, and finally vaults, situated in basement and behind enormous steel doors, said to weigh incredible number of tons and only to be opened by two people working in conjunction. I ask to go inside, and am aghast when I do so by alarming notice on the wall which tells me that If I get shut into the vaults by accident I am not to be alarmed, as there is a supply of air for several hours. Do not at all like the word "several," which is far from being sufficiently specific, and have horrid visions of being shut into the vaults and spending my time there in trying to guess exactly when "several" may be supposed to be drawing to an end. Enquire whether anyone has ever been locked into the vaults, and if they came out mad, but Mr. Lee only replies No one that he has ever heard of, and appears quite unmoved by the idea.

Have often associated banking with callousness, and now perceive how right I was.

Evening is passed agreeably with the Lees

until nine o'clock, when Minnie and parent descend upon us and we all talk about Minnie for about half-an-hour. Take cast-iron resolution before I sleep never to make either of the dear children subjects of long conversations with strangers.

(*Mem:* To let Robert know of this resolution, as feel sure he would approve of it.)

November 13th.—Five o'clock train is selected to take me to Buffalo, and am surprised and relieved to find that I have not got to travel all night, but shall arrive in four-and-a-half hours. Luncheon party is kindly given in my honor by the Lees—Minnie not present, but is again quoted extensively by her mother—and I am asked more than once for opinion on relative merits of Canada and the United States. Can quite see that this is very delicate ground, and have no intention whatever of committing myself to definite statement on the point. Talk instead about English novelists—Kipling evidently very popular, and Hugh Walpole looked upon as interesting new discovery—and I am told by several people that I ought to go to Quebec.

As it is now impossible for me to do so, this leads to very little, beyond repeated assurances from myself that I should *like* to go to Quebec, and am exceedingly sorry not to be going there. One well-informed lady tells me that Harold Nicholson went there and liked it very much. Everybody receives this in respectful silence, and I feel that Harold Nicholson has completely deflated whatever wind there may ever have been in my sails.

Morale is restored later by my host, who takes me aside and says that I have been Just a breath of fresh air from the Old Country, and that I must come again next year. Am touched, and recklessly say that I will. Everyone says good-bye very kindly, and gentleman —hitherto unknown—tells me that he will drive me to the station, as he has to go in that direction later. Minnie's mother heaps coals of fire on my head by telling me that she has a little present for my children, and is going just across the street to get it. This she does, and present turns out to be a Service revolver, which she thinks my boy may like. Can reply with perfect truth that I feel sure of it, and am fortunately not asked for my own reaction; or Robert's.

Revolver, of which I am secretly a good deal afraid, is wedged with the utmost difficulty into the least crowded corner of my attaché-case, and I take my departure.

Rather strange sequel follows a good deal later, when I am having dinner on train and am called out to speak to Customs official. Cannot imagine what he wants me for, and alarming visions of Sing-Sing assail me instantly. Go so far as to decide that I shall try and brief Mr. Clarence Darrow for the defence—but this probably because he is the only American barrister whose name I can remember.

Customs awaits me in the corridor, and looks very grave. Is mine, he enquires, the brown attaché-case under the fur coat in the parlor-car? Yes, it is. Then why, may he ask, do I find it necessary to travel with a revolver? Freakish impulse momentarily assails me, and I nearly—but not quite—reply that I have to do so for the protection of my virtue. Realise in time that this flippancy would be quite out of place, and might very likely land me in

serious trouble, so take wiser and more straightforward course of telling Customs the whole
story of the Service revolver.

He receives it sympathetically, and tells me
that he is a family man himself. (Association
here with Dickens—"I'm a mother myself, Mr.
Copperfulld"—but Customs perhaps not literary, or may prefer Mark Twain, so keep it to
myself.)

Conversation follows, in which I learn names
and ages of the whole family of Customs, and
in return show him small snapshot of Robin
and Vicky with dog Kolynos, playing in the
garden. Customs says That's a fine dog, and
asks what breed, but says nothing about R. and
V. Am slightly disappointed, but have noticed
similar indifference to the children of others on
the part of parents before.

November 13th (continued).—Train, in the
most singular way, arrives at Buffalo ahead of
time. Large and very handsome station receives
me, and I walk about vast hall, which I seem
to have entirely to myself. Red-capped porter,
who is looking after my luggage, seems prepared to remain by it for ever in a fatalistic

kind of way, and receives with indifference my announcement that Someone will be here to meet me by and by.

Can only hope I am speaking the truth, but feel doubtful as time goes on. Presently, however, tall lady in furs appears, and looks all round her, and I say "Dr. Livingstone, I presume?"—but not aloud—and approach her. Am I, I ask, speaking to Mrs. Walker? Lady, in a most uncertain voice, replies No, no—not Mrs. *Walker*. We gaze at one another helplessly and she adds, in a still more uncertain voice: Mrs. Luella White Clarkson. To this I can think of no better reply than Oh, and we walk away from one another in silence, only, however, to meet again repeatedly in our respective perambulations. (Should much like to know what peculiar law governs this state of affairs. Station is perfectly enormous, and practically empty, and neither Mrs. L.W.C. nor myself has the slightest wish ever again to come face to face with one another, yet we seem perfectly unable to avoid doing so. Eventually take to turning my back whenever I see her approaching, and walking smartly in the opposite direction.)

Mental comparison of American and English railway stations follows, and am obliged to admit that America wins hands down. Have never in my life discovered English station that was warm, clean, or quiet, or at which waiting entailed anything but complete physical misery. Compose long letter to Sir Felix Pole on the subject, and have just been publicly thanked by the Lord Mayor of London for ensuing reformations, when I perceive Red-cap making signs. Mrs. Walker—small lady in black, very smart, and no resemblance whatever to Mrs. L.W.C.—has appeared. She apologises very nicely for being late, and I apologise—I hope also very nicely—for the train's having been too early—and we get into her motor which is, as usual, very large and magnificent. (Remarkable contrast between cars to which I am by now becoming accustomed, and ancient Standard so frequently pushed up the hills at home—but have little doubt that I shall be delighted to find myself in old Standard once more.)

Have I, Mrs. Walker instantly enquires,

visited the Niagara Falls? Am obliged to
admit, feeling apologetic, that I have. Thank
God for that, she surprisingly returns. We then
embark on conversation, and I tell her about
Canada, and make rather good story out of
preposterous child Minnie. Mrs. Walker is ap-
preciative, and we get on well.

Buffalo is under snow, and bitterly cold.
House, however, delightfully warm, as usual.
Mrs. Walker hopes that I won't mind a small
room: I perceive that the whole of drawing-
room, dining-room and Robert's study could
easily be fitted inside it, and that it has a bathroom opening out of one end and a sitting-room
the other, and say, Oh no, not in the least.

She then leaves me to rest.

November 14th.—Clothes having emerged
more crumpled than ever from repeated packings, I ask if they could be ironed, and this is
forthwith done by competent maid, who tells
me what I know only too well already, that
best black-and-white evening dress has at one
time been badly stained by coffee, and will
never really look the same again.

Mrs. Walker takes me for a drive, and we

see as much of Buffalo as is compatible with it's being almost altogether under snow, and she asks me rather wistfully if I can tell her anything about celebrated English woman-novelist who once stayed with her for a fortnight and was charming, but has never answered any letters since. Am disgusted with the ingratitude of my distinguished country-woman, and invent explanations about her having been ill, and probably forbidden by the doctor to attend to any correspondence whatever.

Mrs. Walker receives this without demur, but wears faintly cynical expression, and am by no means convinced that she has been taken in by it, especially as she tells me later on that when in London a year ago she rang up distinguished novelist, who had apparently great difficulty in remembering who she was. Feel extremely ashamed of this depth of ingratitude, contrast it with extraordinary kindness and hospitality proffered to English visitors by American hosts, and hope that someone occasionally returns some of it.

Become apprehensive towards afternoon,

when Mrs. W. tells me that the Club at which
I am to lecture has heard all the best-known
European speakers, at one time or another, and
is composed of highly-cultivated members.

Revise my lecture frantically, perceive that
it is totally lacking in cultivation, or even ordinary evidence of intelligence, and ask Mrs. W.
whether she doesn't think the Club would like
a reading instead. Have no real hope that this
will succeed, nor does it. Nothing for it but to
put on my newly-ironed blue, powder my nose,
and go.

Mrs. W. is considerate, and does not attempt
conversation on the way, except when she once
says that she hopes I can eat oysters. Feel it
highly improbable that I shall ever be able to
eat anything again, and hear myself muttering
for sole reply: "Who knows but the world may
end to-night?"

World, needless to say, does not end, and
I have to pull myself together, meet a great
many Club members—alert expressions and
very expensive clothes—and subsequently
mount small platform on which stand two
chairs, table and reading-desk.

Elderly lady in grey takes the chair—reminds me of Robert's Aunt Eleanor, but cannot say why—and says that she is not going to speak for more than a few moments. Everyone, she knows, is looking forward to hearing something far more interesting than any words of *hers* can be. At this she glances benevolently towards me, and I smile modestly, and wish I could drop down in a fit and be taken away on the spot. Instead, I have presently to get on to my feet, and adjust small sheet of notes—now definitely looking crumpled and dirty—on to reading-desk.

Head, as usual, gets very hot, and feet very cold, and am badly thrown off my balance by very ancient lady who sits in the front row and holds her hand to her ear throughout, as if unable to hear a word I utter. This, however, evidently not the case, as she comes up afterwards and tells me that she was one of the Club's original members, and has never missed a single lecture. Offer her my congratulations on this achievement, and then wish I hadn't, as it sounds conceited, and add that I hope she has found it worth the trouble. She replies

[146]

*Am badly thrown off my balance by very ancient lady
who sits in the front row*

rather doubtfully Yes—on the whole, Yes—and refers to André Maurois. *His* lecture was positively brilliant. I reply, truthfully, that I feel sure it was, and we part. Aunt Eleanor and I exchange polite speeches—I meet various ladies, one of whom tells me that she knows a great friend of mine. Rose, I suggest? No, not Rose. Dear Katherine Ellen Blatt, who is at present in New York, but hopes to be in Boston when I am. She has, says the lady, a perfectly lovely personality. And she has been saying the most wonderful things about *me*. Try to look more grateful than I really feel, over this.

(*Query:* Does not public life, even on a small scale, distinctly lead in the direction of duplicity? *Answer:* Unfortunately, Yes.)

Aunt Eleanor now approaches and says—as usual—that she knows an English woman can't do without her tea, and that some is now awaiting me. Am touched by this evidence of thoughtfulness, and drink tea—which is much too strong—and eat cinnamon toast, to which I am by no means accustomed, and which re-

[147]

minds me very painfully of nauseous drug frequently administered to Vicky by Mademoiselle.

Conversation with Aunt Eleanor ensues. She
does not, herself, write books, she says, but
those who do have always had a strange fasci-
nation for her. She has often *thought* of writing a book—many of her friends have implored
her to do so, in fact—but no, she finds it impossible to begin. And yet, there are many
things in her life about which whole, entire
novels might well be written. Everybody de-
votes a moment of rather awed silence to
conjecturing the nature of Aunt Eleanor's singular experiences, and anti-climax is felt to have
ensued when small lady in rather frilly frock
suddenly announces in a pipy voice that she
has a boy-cousin, living in Oklahoma, who once
wrote something for *The New Yorker*, but they
didn't ever publish it.

This more or less breaks up the party, and
Mrs. Walker drives me home again, and says
in a rather exhausted way that she thanks
Heaven that's over.

We talk about Aunt Eleanor—she has been
twice married, one husband died and the other

one left her, but no divorce—and she has two daughters but neither of them live at home. Can quite understand it, and say so. Mrs. Walker assents mildly, which encourages me to add that I didn't take to Aunt Eleanor much. No, says Mrs. Walker thoughtfully, she doesn't really think that Aunt E. and I would ever get on together very well.

Am quite surprised and hurt at this, and realise that, though I am quite prepared to dislike Aunt Eleanor, I find it both unjust and astonishing that she should be equally repelled by me. Rather interesting side-light on human nature thrown here, and have dim idea of going into the whole thing later, preferably with Rose—always so well-informed—or dear Mary Kellway, full of intelligence, even though unable to write legibly—but this probably owing to stress of life in country parish, so much more crowded with activities than any other known form of existence.

Dinner-party closes the day, and I put on backless evening dress, add coatee, take coatee off again, look at myself with mirror and hand-glass in conjunction, resume coatee, and retain it for the rest of the evening.

November 15th.—Weather gets colder and colder as I approach Boston, and this rouses prejudice in me, together with repeated assurances from everybody I meet to the effect that Boston is the most English town in America, and I shall simply adore it. Feel quite unlike adoration as train takes me through snowy country, and affords glimpses of towns that appear to be entirely composed of Gasoline Stations and Motion-Picture Theatres. Towards nine o'clock in the morning, I have an excellent breakfast—food in America definitely a very bright spot—and return to railway-carriage where I see familiar figure, hat still worn at very dashing angle, and recognise Pete. Feel as if I had met my oldest friend, in the middle of a crowd of strangers, and we greet one another cordially. Pete tells me that I seem to be standing up to it pretty well—which I take to be a compliment to my powers of endurance —and unfolds terrific programme of the activities he has planned for me in Boston.

Assent to everything, but add that the thing

I want to do most of all, is to visit the Alcott House at Concord, Mass. At this Pete looks astounded, and replies that this is, he supposes, merely a personal fancy, and so far as he knows no time for anything of that kind has been allowed in the schedule. Am obliged to agree that it probably hasn't, but repeat that I really want to do that more than anything else in America. (Much later on, compose eloquent and convincing speech, to the effect that I have worked very hard and done all that was required of me, and that I am fully entitled to gratify my own wishes for one afternoon at least. Am quite clear that if I had only said all this at the time, Pete would have been left without a leg to stand upon. Unfortunately, however, I do not do so.)

Boston is reached—step out of the train into the iciest cold that it has ever been my lot to encounter—and am immediately photographed by unknown man carrying camera and unpleasant little light-bulb which he flashes unexpectedly into my eyes. No one makes the slightest comment on this proceeding, and am convinced that he has mistaken me for somebody quite different.

Two young creatures from the *Boston Transcript* meet me, and enquire, more or less instantly, what I feel about the Problem of the American Woman, but Pete, with great good feeling, suggests that we should discuss it all in taxi on our way to Hotel, which we do. One of them then hands me a cable—(announcing death of Robin or Vicky?)—and says it arrived this morning.

Cable says, in effect, that I must at all costs get into touch with Caroline Concannon's dear friend and cousin Mona, who lives in Pinckney Street, would love to meet me, has been written to, everything all right at flat, love from Caroline.

Am quite prepared to get into touch with dear friend and cousin, but say nothing to Pete about it, for fear of similar disconcerting reaction to that produced by suggestion of visiting Alcott House.

Am conducted to nice little Hotel in Charles Street, and told once by Pete, and twice by each of the *Boston Transcript* young ladies, that I am within a stone's throw of the Common. Chief association with the Common is *An Old-Fashioned Girl*, in which heroine goes tobogganing, but do not refer to this, and merely reply that That is very nice. So it may be, but not at the moment when Common, besides being deep in snow, is quite evidently being searched from end to end by ice-laden north-east wind.

Pete, with firmness to which I am by now accustomed, says that he will leave me to unpack but come and fetch me again in an hour's time, to visit customary bookshops.

Telephone bell in sitting-room soon afterwards rings, and it appears that dear Rose—like Caroline Concannon—has a friend in Boston, and that the friend is downstairs and proposes to come up right away and see me. I say Yes, Yes, and I shall be delighted, and hastily shut suit-cases which I have this moment opened, and look at myself in the glass instead.

Results of this inspection are far from encouraging, but nothing can be done about it now, and can only concentrate on trying to

[153]

remember everything that Rose has ever told me about her Boston friend, called, I believe, Fanny Mason. Sum total of my recollections is that the friend is very literary, and has written a good deal, and travelled all over the world, and is very critical.

Am rather inclined to become agitated by all this, but friend appears, and has the good feeling to keep these disquieting attributes well out of sight, and concentrate on welcoming me very kindly to Boston—(exactly like England and all English people always love it on that account)—and enquiring affectionately about Rose. (Am disgusted to learn from what she says that dear Rose has written to her far more recently, as well as at much greater length, than to myself. Shall have a good deal to say to Rose, when we meet again.)

Friend then announces that she has A Girl downstairs. The Girl has brought a car, and is going to show me Boston this morning, take me to lunch at a Women's Club, and to a tea later. This more than kind, but also definitely disconcerting in view of arrangements made by

Pete, and I say O Miss Mason—and then stop, rather like heroine of a Victorian novel.

Miss M. at once returns that I must not dream of calling her anything but Fanny. She has heard of me for years and years, and we are already old friends. This naturally calls for thanks and acknowledgements on my part, and I then explain that publishers' representative is in Boston, and calling for me in an hour's time, which I'm afraid means that I cannot take advantage of kind offer.

Miss M.—Fanny—undefeated, and says it is Important that I should see Boston, no one who has not done so can be said to know anything whatever about America, and The Girl is waiting for me downstairs. Suggest—mostly in order to gain time—that The Girl should be invited to come up, and this is done by telephone.

She turns out to be very youthful and good-looking blonde, introduced to me as "Leslie"— (first names evidently the fashion in Boston) —and evidently prepared to take me anywhere in the world, more or less, at any moment.

Explain all over again about Pete and the

booksellers. Fanny remains adamant, but
Leslie says reasonably: What about to-morrow
instead, and I advance cherished scheme for
visiting Alcott House. This, it appears, is
fraught with difficulties, as Alcott House is
impenetrably shut at this time of year. Feel
that if Pete comes to hear of this, my last hope
is gone. Leslie looks rather sorry for me, and
says perhaps something could be arranged, but
anyway I had better come out now and see
Boston. Fanny is also urgent on this point, and
I foresee deadlock, when telephone rings and
Pete is announced, and is told to come upstairs.

Brilliant idea then strikes me, I introduce
everybody, and tell Pete that there has been
rather a clash of arrangements, but that doubtless he and Miss Mason can easily settle it
between themselves. Will they, in the meanwhile, excuse me, as I positively must see about
my unpacking? Retreat firmly into the bedroom
to do so, but spend some of the time with ear
glued to the wall, trying to ascertain whether
Pete and Miss M.—both evidently very strong
personalities—are going to fly at one another's
throats or not. Voices are certainly definitely

Tell Pete . . . that doubtless he and Miss Mason
can easily settle it between themselves

raised, usually both at once, but nothing more formidable happens, and I hope that physical violence may be averted.

Decide that on the whole I am inclined to back Pete, as possessing rock-like quality of immovability once his mind is made up—doubtless very useful asset in dealing with authors, publishers, and so on.

Subsequent events prove that I am right, and Pete walks me to bookshop, with laconic announcement to Leslie and Miss M.—Fanny— that I shall be at their disposal by 12.30.

November 16th.—Most extraordinary revolution in everybody's outlook—excepting my own—by communication from Mr. Alexander Woollcott. He has, it appears, read in a paper (*Boston Transcript?*) that my whole object in coming to America was to visit the Alcott House, and of this he approves to such an extent that he is prepared to Mention It in a Radio Talk, if I will immediately inform him of my reactions to the expedition.

Entire *volte-face* now takes place in attitude of Pete, Fanny, and everybody else. If Alexander Woollcott thinks I ought to visit

[157]

Alcott House, it apparently becomes essential
that I should do so and Heaven and earth must,
if necessary, be moved in order to enable me to.
Am much impressed by the remarkable difference between enterprise that I merely want to
undertake for my own satisfaction, and the
same thing when it is advocated by Mr. A.W.

Result of it all is that the members of the
Alcott-Pratt family are approached, they respond with the greatest kindness, and offer to
open the house especially for my benefit, Fanny
says that Leslie will drive me out to Concord
on Sunday afternoon, and she will herself ac-
company us, not in order to view Alcott House
—she does not want to see it, which rather
shocks me—but to visit a relation of her own
living there. Pete does not associate himself
personally with the expedition, as he will by
that time have gone to New York, Charlestown,
Oshkosh, or some other distant spot—but it
evidently meets with his warmest approval,
and his last word to me is an injunction to take
paper and pencil with me and send account of
my impressions red-hot to Mr. Alexander
Woollcott.

November 18th.—Go to see football game,
Harvard *v.* Army. Am given to understand—
and can readily believe—that this is a privilege
for which Presidents, Crowned Heads, and
Archbishops would one and all give ten years of
life at the very least. It has only been obtained
for me by the very greatest exertions on the
part of everybody.

Fanny says that I shall be frozen—(can
well believe it)—but that it will be worth it,
and Leslie thinks I may find it rather difficult
to follow—but it will be worth it—and they
both agree that there is always a risk of pneumonia in this kind of weather. Wonder if they
are going to add that it will still be worth it,
because if so, shall disagree with them forcibly
—but they heap coals of fire on my head for
this unworthy thought by offering to lend me
rugs, furs, mufflers, and overshoes. Escort has
been provided for me in the person of an admirer of Fanny's—name unknown to me from
first to last—and we set out together at one
o'clock. Harvard stadium is enormous—no
roof, which I think a mistake—and we sit in
open air, and might be comfortable if tempera-

ture would only rise above zero. Fanny's admirer is extremely kind to me, and can only
hope he isn't thinking all the time how much
pleasanter it would be if he were only escorting
Fanny instead.

(Reminiscence here of once-popular song:
"I am dancing with tears in my eyes, 'Cos the
girl in my arms isn't you." Have always felt
this attitude rather hard on girl actually being
danced with at the moment of singing.)

Ask questions that I hope sound fairly intelligent, and listen attentively to the answers.
Escort in return then paralyses me by putting
to me various technical points in regard to what
he calls the English Game. Try frantically to
recall everything that I can ever remember
having heard from Robin, but am only able to
recollect that he once said Soccer was absolutely lousy and that I rebuked him for it.
Translate this painful reminiscence into civilised version to the effect that Rugger is more
popular than Soccer with Our Schoolboys.

Presently a mule appears and is ridden round
the field by a member of one team or the other
—am not sure which—and I observe, idioti-

cally, that It's like a Rodeo—and immediately perceive that it isn't in the least, and wish I hadn't spoken. Fortunately a number of young gentlemen in white suddenly emerge on to the ground, turn beautiful back somersaults in perfect unison, and cheer madly through a megaphone. Am deeply impressed, and assure Fanny's admirer that we have nothing in the least like that at Wembley, Twickenham, nor, so far as I know, anywhere else. He agrees, very solemnly, that the cheers are a Great Feature of the Game.

Soon afterwards we really get started, and I watch my first game of American football. Players all extensively padded and vast numbers of substitute-players wait about in order to rush in and replace them when necessary. Altogether phenomenal number of these exchanges takes place, but as no stretchers visible, conclude that most of the injuries received fall short of being mortal.

Fanny's admirer gives me explanations about what is taking place from time to time, but is apt to break off in the middle of a phrase when excitement overcomes him. Other interruptions

[161]

are occasioned by organised yellings and roarings, conducted from the field, in which the spectators join.

At about four o'clock it is said to be obvious that Harvard hasn't got a chance, and soon afterwards the Army is declared to have won.

Escort and I look at each other and say Well, and Wasn't it marvellous, and then stand up and I discover that I am quite unable to feel my feet at all, and that all circulation in the rest of my body has apparently stopped altogether—probably frozen.

We totter as best we can through the crowd —escort evidently just as cold as I am, judging by the color of his face and hands—and over bridge, past buildings that I am told are all part of the College, and to flat with attractive view across the river. As I have not been warned by anybody that this is in store, I remain unaware throughout why I am being entertained there, or by whom. Hot tea, for once, is extraordinarily welcome, and so is superb log-fire; and I talk to unknown, but agreeable, American about President Roosevelt, the state of the dollar—we both take a gloomy view of this—and extreme beauty of American foliage in the woods of Maine—where I have never set foot, but about which I have heard a good deal.

November 19th.—Expedition to Concord—now smiled upon by all, owing to intervention of dear Alexander W.—takes place, and definitely ranks in my own estimation higher than anything else I have done in America.

All is snow, silence and loveliness, with frame-houses standing amongst trees, and no signs of either picture-houses, gasoline-stations, or hot-dog stalls. Can think of nothing but *Little Women*, and visualise scene after scene from well-remembered and beloved book. Fanny, sympathetic, but insensible to appeal of *Little Women*, is taken on to see her relations, and I remain with Mrs. Pratt, surviving relative of Miss Alcott, and another elderly lady, both kind and charming, and prepared to show me everything there is to see.

Could willingly remain there for hours and hours.

Time, however, rushes by with its usual speed when I am absorbed and happy, and I

[163]

am obliged to make my farewells, collect post-cards and pictures with which I have most kindly been presented, and book given me for Vicky which I shall, I know, be seriously tempted to keep for myself.

Can think of nothing but the March family for the remainder of the day, and am much annoyed at being reminded by Fanny and Leslie that whatever happens, I must send my impressions to Mr. Alexander Woollcott without delay.

November 20th.—Just as day of my departure from Boston arrives, weather relents and suddenly becomes quite mild. I go and call on Caroline Concannon's friend, and am much taken with her. She has no party, which is a great relief, and we talk about England and C.C. Very amusing and good company, says the friend, and I agree, and add that Caroline is looking after my flat during my absence. Slight misgiving crosses my mind as to the literal accuracy of this statement, but this perhaps ungenerous, and make amends by saying that she is Very Good with Children—which is perfectly true.

Walk back across Common, and see very pretty brick houses, Queen Anne style. Old mauve glass in many window panes, but notice cynically that these always appear in ground-floor windows, where they can be most easily admired by the passers-by.

Decide that this is certainly a good moment for taking Rose's advice to buy myself a Foundation Garment in America, as they understand these things, says Rose, much better than we do in England. I accordingly enter a shop and find elderly saleswoman, who disconcerts me by saying in a sinister way that I certainly can't wear the ordinary suspender-belt, that's very evident. She supplies me with one that is, I suppose, removed from the ordinary, and her last word is an injunction to me not to forget that whatever I do, I mustn't wear an ordinary belt. It'll be the complete ruin of my figure if I do. Depart, in some dejection.

Shock awaits me on return to Hotel when I discover that Miss Katherine Ellen Blatt has just arrived, and has sent up a note to my room to say so. It will, she writes, be so delightful to meet again, she revelled in our last

[165]

delightful talk and is longing for another. Entertain myself for some little while in composing imaginary replies to this, but candor, as usual, is obliged to give way to civility, and I write very brief reply suggesting that K.E.B. and I should meet in the hall for a moment before my train leaves, when she, Fanny Mason —whom she doubtless knows already—and Leslie, will all be privileged to see one another.

Customary pre-occupation with my appearance follows, and I go in search of hotel beauty-parlor. Intelligent young operator deals with me, and says that one of her fellow-workers is also British and would be very happy to meet me. My English accent, she adds thoughtfully, is a prettier one than hers. This definitely no over-statement, as fellow-worker turns out to be from Huddersfield and talks with strong North-country accent.

On return to ground-floor—hair at least clean and wavy—Miss Blatt materialises. She greets me as an old and dear friend and tells me that one or two perfectly lovely women of her acquaintance are just crazy to meet me, and are coming to a Tea in the hotel this very afternoon in order that they may have the pleasure of doing so.

I thank her, express gratification and regret, and explain firmly that I am going on to Washington this afternoon. Oh, returns Miss Blatt very blithely indeed, I don't have to give that a thought. She has taken it up with my publishers by telephone, and they quite agree with her that the contacts she has arranged for me are very, very important, and I can easily make the ten-thirty train instead of the six, and reach Washington in plenty of time.

All presence of mind deserts me, and I say Yes, and Very Well, to everything, and soon afterwards find myself suggesting that Miss Blatt should lunch at my table.

(*Query:* Why? *Answer:* comes there none.)

Lunch proves definitely informative: Miss Blatt tells me about dear Beverley Nichols, who has just sent her a copy of his new book, and dear Anne Parrish, who hasn't yet sent a copy of hers, but is certainly going to do so. I say Yes, and How Splendid, and wonder what Miss Blatt can be like when she is all by herself, with no celebrities within miles, and no telephone. Strange idea crosses my mind that in such circumstances she would probably hardly exist as a personality at all, and might actually dissolve into nothingness. Something almost metaphysical in this train of thought, and am rather impressed by it myself, but cannot, naturally, ask Miss Blatt to share in my admiration.

Talk to her instead about murder stories, which I like, and instance Mrs. Belloc-Lowndes as a favorite of mine. Miss Blatt says No, murder stories make no appeal to her whatever, but Mrs. Belloc-Lowndes—Marie—is one of her very dearest friends. So is another Marie, —Queen of Roumania. So, oddly enough, is Marie Tempest.

On this note we part, before K.E.B. has time to think of anybody else whose name happens to be Marie.

Am obliged to extract red frock from suitcase, in which I have already carefully folded it—but perhaps not as carefully as I hoped, as it comes out distinctly creased—and put it on in honor of Miss Blatt's tea. This duly takes place, and is handsomely attended. Miss B. no doubt as well-known in Boston as in New York, London, Paris and Hongkong. Am gratified at seeing Caroline C's charming friend, and should like to talk to her, but am given no opportunity.

Very large lady in black pins me into a corner, tells me to sit down, and takes her seat beside me on small sofa. She then tells me all about a local literary society, of which she is herself the foundress and the president, called the Little Thinkers. (Can only hope that in original days when name of club was chosen, this may have been less ironical than it is now.) President—hope with all my heart that she hasn't guessed my thoughts—adds that they chose to call themselves Little Thinkers because it indicated modesty. They are none of them, she explains, really Deep and Profound —not like Darwin or Huxley—(I make effort —not good—to look surprised and incredulous at this)—But they all like to *think*, and to ask themselves questions. They read, if she may say so, very deeply. And they meet and Discuss Things every Tuesday afternoon. Had I been staying here rather longer, says President, the

[169]

Little Thinkers would have been only too pleased to invite me as Guest of Honor to one of their meetings, and perhaps I would have given them a short talk on the Real Meaning of Life.

Should like to reply flippantly: Perhaps and Perhaps Not—but President of the Little Thinkers evidently no good subject for wit of this description, so express instead respectful regret that time will not allow me to avail myself of the suggested privilege.

Moment, it now seems to me, has definitely arrived for both the President of the L. T.'s and myself to move gracefully away from one another and each talk to somebody else. This turns out to be not easy of accomplishment, as President is between me and the rest of the world, and seems not to know how to get away, though am morally convinced that she would give quite a lot to be able to do so. We continue to look at one another and to say the same things over and over again in slightly different words, and I see Katherine Ellen Blatt eyeing me rather severely from the far end of the room, and evidently feeling—with justice—

[170]

that I am not doing my fair share towards making a success of the party.

At last become desperate, say Well, in a frantic way, and rise to my feet. President of the L. T.'s immediately leaps to hers—looking unspeakably relieved—and we exchange apologetic smiles and turn our backs on one another.

(*Mem:* Surely very interesting statistics might be collected with regard to the number of such social problems and varying degrees of difficulty with which these can, or cannot, be solved? Would willingly contribute small *exposé* of my own, to any such symposium. *Query:* Approach Lord Beaverbrook on the point, or not? Sunday papers frequently very dull, and topics raised by correspondents often tedious to the last degree.)

Catch the eye of Caroline C's friend, Mona, and am delighted and prepare to go and talk to her, but Miss Blatt immediately stops me and says that I must meet a very old friend of hers, Mr. Joseph Ross, who has lived for fifty-three years in America.

Take this to imply that he once lived somewhere else, and after a few words have no difficulty in guessing that this was Scotland. Refer to it rather timidly—who knows what reasons Mr. J.R. may have had for leaving his native land—but he tells me rather disconcertingly that he goes home once in every two years, and merely lives in America because the climate suits him. I say Yes, it's very dry, and we both look out of the window, and Mr. Joseph Ross —rather to my relief—is taken away from me by a strange lady, who smiles at me winningly and says that I mustn't mind, as millions of people are just waiting for a chance to talk to me, and it isn't fair of Uncle Joe to monopolise me. Am struck by this flattering, if inaccurate, way of putting it, and look nervously round for the millions, but can see no sign of any of them.

Make another effort to reach Caroline's friend, and this time am successful. She smiles, and looks very pretty, and says that Caroline never writes to her but she sometimes gets news through Jane and Maurice. Do I know Jane and Maurice and the twins?

Am obliged to disclaim any knowledge of any of them, but add madly that I do so wish

I *did*. Friend receives this better than it deserves, and we are just going happily into the question of mutual acquaintances when the President of the Little Thinkers recrudesces, and says that She wants to have me meet one of their very brightest members, Mrs. Emily Dowling Dean. Mrs. Emily Dowling Dean is a Southerner by birth and has a perfectly wonderful Southern accent.

Caroline's friend melts away and Mrs. Emily Dowling Dean and I confront one another, and she tells me that Boston is a very English town, and that she herself comes from the South and that people tell her she has never lost her Southern accent. She is—as usual—extremely agreeable to look at, and I reflect dejectedly that all the women in America are either quite young and lovely, or else quite old and picturesque. Ordinary female middle-age, so prevalent in European countries, apparently non-existent over here. (Katherine Ellen Blatt an exception to this rule, but probably much older than she looks. Or perhaps much younger? Impossible to say.)

Party draws to a close—discover that, as

usual, I have a sore throat from trying to scream as loud as everybody else is screaming —and Fanny Mason kindly extracts me from saying good-bye and takes me up to my room, —which I shall have to leave only too soon for the station.

Take the opportunity of writing letters to Robert and to each of the children. Am obliged to print in large letters for Vicky, and this takes time, as does endeavor to be reasonably legible for Robin's benefit. Robert's letter comes last, and is definitely a scrawl. (Wish I had judged Mary Kellway rather less severely.)

Am seen off at station by Fanny, Leslie, Katherine Ellen Blatt, and three unidentified men—probably admirers of Fanny and Leslie. One of them, quite gratuitously and much to my surprise and gratification, presents me with large and handsome book, called *American Procession*, for the journey.

Train departs—extraordinary and unpleasant jerk that I have noticed before in American trains, and which I think reflects ill on their engine-drivers—and I look at *American Procession*, which is full of photographs and

*President of The Little Thinkers . . . wants to have
me meet one of their very brightest members*

extremely interesting. Am, however, depressed
to realise that I can quite well remember most
of the incidents depicted, and that fashions
which now appear wholly preposterous were
worn by myself in youth and even early middle
life.

Retire to bed, under the usual difficulties,
behind curtain—always so reminiscent of film-
stories—though nothing could be less like
heroines there depicted than I am myself.

November 21st. Immense relief to find Washington very much warmer than Boston, even
at crack of dawn. Nobody meets me, at which
I am slightly relieved owing to rather disastrous
effect of curtailed sleep on complexion and
appearance generally, and I proceed by taxi to
Hotel indicated by Pete. General impression as
I go that Washington is very clean and pretty,
with numbers of dazzlingly white buildings.
Am rather disposed to feel certain that every
house I see in turn must be the White House.
Hotel is colossal building of about thirty-five
stories, with three wings, and complete platoon
of negro porters in pale blue uniforms standing
at the entrance. Find myself at once thinking

of *Uncle Tom's Cabin*, and look compassionately at porters, but am bound to say they all seem perfectly cheerful and prosperous.

Rather disconcerting reception at the desk in office follows. The clerk is extremely sorry, but the hotel is absolutely full up. Not a bedroom anywhere. We look at one another rather blankly, and I feebly mention name of extremely distinguished publishing firm by which I have been directed to come here and not elsewhere. That don't make a mite of difference, says the clerk, shaking his head. He's just as sorry as he can be, but not *a* bed is available. Very well. I resign myself. But as I am a complete stranger, perhaps he will very kindly tell me where I can go next? Oh yes, says the clerk, looking infinitely relieved, he can easily do that. The Wardman-Park Hotel will be tickled to death to have me go there. He will 'phone up right away and make the reservation for me, if I like. Accept this gratefully, and in a moment all is settled, and blue-uniformed darkie has put me and my luggage into another taxi, after I have gratefully thanked hotel-clerk and he has assured me that I am very

[176]

welcome. (This perhaps slightly ironical in the circumstances—but evidently not intended to be so.)

Wardman-Park Hotel also turns out to be enormous and reflection assails me that if I am also told here that Every room is full up, I shall definitely be justified in coming to the conclusion that there is something about my appearance which suggests undesirability. Am, however, spared this humiliation. Wardman-Park—negroes this time in crushed-strawberry-color—receives me with affability, and accommodates me with room on the fifteenth floor.

I unpack—dresses creased as usual, and I reflect for the thousandth time that I shall never make a good packer, and that continual practice is, if anything, making me worse—and go down to breakfast. Excellent coffee starts, not for the first time, rather melancholy train of thought concerning Cook, and her utter inability to produce even moderately drinkable coffee. Shall make a point of telling her how much I have enjoyed *all* coffee in America.

(*Query:* Is this a cast-iron resolution, to be put into effect directly I get home in whatever

[177]

mood I may happen to find Cook—or is it merely one of those rhetorical flashes, never destined to be translated into action? *Answer:* All too probably: The latter.)

Reflect with satisfaction that I can actually claim friendship with official in the State Department, met several times in London, and whom I now propose to ring up on the telephone as soon as the day is respectably advanced. Recollect that I liked him very much, and hope that this may still hold good after lapse of five years, and may also extend to newly-acquired wife, whom I have never met, and that neither of them will take a dislike to me.

(*Query:* Has rebuff at first Hotel visited slightly un-nerved me? If so, *morale* will doubtless be restored by breakfast. Order more coffee and a fresh supply of toast on the strength of this thought.)

Greatly surprised as I leave dining-room to find myself presented with small card on which is printed name hitherto totally unknown to me: General Clarence Dove. I say to the waiter —not very intelligently—What is this? and

he refrains from saying, as he well might, that
It's a visiting-card, and replies instead that It's
the gentleman at the table near the door.

At this I naturally look at the table near
the door, and elderly gentleman with bald
head and rather morose expression makes half-
hearted movement towards getting up, and
bows. I bow in return, and once more scruti-
nise card, but it still looks exactly the same,
and I am still equally unable to wake any
association in connection with General Clarence
Dove. Feel constrained to take one or two steps
towards him, which courtesy he handsomely
returns by standing up altogether and throwing
his table napkin on the floor.

Cannot help wishing the waiter would put
things on a more solid basis by introducing us,
but this feeling probably only a manifestation
of British snobbishness, and nothing of the
kind occurs. Elderly gentleman, however, rises
to the occasion more or less, and tells me that
he has been written to by Mrs. Wheelwright,
of Long Island, and told to look out for me,
and that I am writing a book about America.

He has therefore ventured to make himself known to me.

Express my gratification, and beg him to go on with his breakfast. This he refuses to do, and says—obviously untruly—that he has finished, but that we could perhaps take a little turn together in the sunshine. This hope rather optimistic, as sunshine—though present—turns out to be of poor quality, and we hastily retire to spacious hall, furnished with alternate arm-chairs and ashtrays on stands. Central heating, undeniably, far more satisfactory than sun-shine, at this time of year, but doubtful if this thought would appeal to General Clarence Dove—aspect rather forbidding—so keep it to myself.

Just as I am preparing to make agreeable speech anent the beauties of Washington, the General utters.

He hears, he says, that I am writing a book about America. Now, he may be old-fashioned, but personally he finds this rather difficult to understand.

I say, No, no, in great agitation, and explain that I am *not* writing a book about America, that I shouldn't ever dream of doing such a thing, after a six months' visit, and that on the contrary . . .

A book about America, says the General, without paying the slightest attention to my eloquence, is not a thing to be undertaken in that spirit at all. Far too many British and other writers have made this mistake. They come over—whether invited or not—and are received by many of the best people in America, and what do they do in return? I again break in and say that I know, and I have often thought what a pity it is, and the last thing I should ever dream of doing would be to . . .

Besides, interrupts the General, quite un-moved, America is a large country. A very large country indeed. To write a book about it would be a very considerable task. What people don't seem to understand is that no person can call themselves qualified to write a book about it after a mere superficial visit lasting less than two months.

Am by now almost frantic, and reiterate in a subdued shriek that I agree with every word the General is saying, and have always thought exactly the same thing—but all is in vain. He continues to look straight in front of him, and to assure me that there can be no greater mistake than to come over to a country like America, spend five minutes there, and then rush home and write a book about it. Far too many people have done this already.

Can see by now that it is completely useless to try and persuade General Clarence Dove that I am not amongst these, and have no intention of ever being so—and I therefore remain silent whilst he says the same things all over again about five times more.

After this he gets up, assures me that it has been a pleasure to meet me, and that he will certainly read my book about America when it comes out, and we part—never, I hope, to meet again.

Am completely shattered by this extraordinary encounter for several hours afterwards, but eventually summon up enough strength to ring up Department of State—which makes me feel important—and get into touch with friend James. He responds most agreeably, sounds flatteringly pleased at my arrival, and invites me to lunch with himself and his wife and his baby.

Baby?

Oh yes, he has a daughter aged two months. Very intelligent. I say, quite truthfully, that I should love to see her, and feel that she will be a much pleasanter companion than General Clarence Dove—and much more on my own conversational level into the bargain.

James later fetches me by car, and we drive to his apartment situated in street rather strangely named O. Street. I tell him that he hasn't altered in the very least—he says the same, though probably with less truth, about me, and enquires after Robert, the children, Kolynos the dog—now, unfortunately, no longer with us—and Helen Wills the cat. I then meet his wife, Elizabeth—very pretty and attractive—and his child, Katherine—not yet pretty, but I like her and am gratified because she doesn't cry when I pick her up—and we have peaceful and pleasant lunch.

Conversation runs on personal and domestic lines, and proves thoroughly congenial after recent long spell of social and literary exer-

tions. Moreover *Anthony Adverse motif* entirely absent, which is a relief.

Reluctantly leave this agreeable atmosphere
in order to present myself at Department
Store, in accordance with explicit instructions
received from Pete.

Arrange, however, to go with James next day
and be shown house of George Washington.

Store is, as usual, large and important, and
I enter it with some trepidation, and very
nearly walk straight out again on catching sight
of large and flattering photograph of myself,
taken at least three years ago, propped up in
prominent position. Printed notice below says
that I am Speaking at Four O'clock this afternoon.

Memory transports me to village at home,
and comparative frequency with which I Speak,
alternatively with Our Vicar's Wife, at
Women's Institute, Mother's Union, and the
like organisations, and total absence of excitement with which both of us are alike hailed.
Fantastic wonder crosses my mind as to whether
photograph, exhibited beforehand, say in Post

Office window, would be advisable, but on further reflection decide against this.

(Photograph was taken in Bond Street, head and shoulders only, and can distinctly recollect that Vicky, on seeing it, enquired in horrified tones if I was *all* naked?)

Enquire for book department, am told to my confusion that I am in it, and realise with horror that I am, but have been completely lost in idiotic and unprofitable reverie. Make no attempt to explain myself, but simply ask for Mrs. Roberta Martin, head of department. She appears—looks about twenty-five but is presumably more—and welcomes me very kindly.

Would I like tea *before* I speak, or *after*?

She asks this so nicely that I am impelled to candor, and say that I wouldn't really like tea at all, but could we have a cup of coffee together afterwards?

We could, and do.

Find ourselves talking about boys. Mrs. R. M. says she has a son of fourteen, which I find quite incredible, and very nearly tell her so, but am restrained by sudden obscure association with extraordinary behavior of General Clarence Dove.

Boys a great responsibility, we agree, but very nice. Her Sidney and my Robin have points in common. Did Sidney like parties in early childhood? No, not at all. Wild horses wouldn't drag him to one. Am relieved to hear it, especially when his mother adds that It All Came Later.

Have vision of Robin, a year or two hence, clamoring for social life. (Probably finding it very difficult to get, now I come to think of it, as neighborhood anything but populous.)

Time, with all this, passes very agreeably, and Mrs. Roberta Martin and I part with mutual esteem and liking.

Take a look round various departments as I go out, and see several things I should like to buy, but am already doubtful if funds are going to hold out till return to New York, so restrict myself to small sponge, pad of note-paper, and necklace of steel beads that I think may appeal to Mademoiselle and go with her Grey.

November 22nd.—Home of George Washing-

Enquire where historical cherry-tree can be seen

ton inspected, and am much moved by its beauty. Enquire where historical cherry-tree can be seen, but James replies—surely rather cynically?—that cherry-tree episode now practically discredited altogether. Find this hard to believe.

(*Mem:* Say nothing about it at home. Story of George W. and cherry-tree not infrequently useful as illustration when pointing out to dear Vicky the desirability of strict truthfulness. Moreover, entire story always most popular when playing charades.)

On leaving George Washington, we proceed to home of General Robert E. Lee, but unfortunately arrive there too late and have to content ourselves with pressing our noses against the windows. Subsequently miss the way, in terrific maze of avenues that surround the house, find gate at last and discover that it is locked, have visions of staying there all night, but subsequently unfastened gate is reached, and we safely emerge.

James shows me the Lincoln Memorial, and I definitely think it the most beautiful thing, without exception, that I have seen in America.

[187]

Tour is concluded by a drive through Washington, and I see the outside of a good many Embassies, and am reluctantly obliged to conclude that the British one is far indeed from being the most beautiful amongst them. Decide that the Japanese one is the prettiest.

Evening spent with James and Elizabeth. Katherine still engaging, but slightly inclined to scream when left alone in bedroom. (Am forcibly reminded of dear Robin's very early days.)

Leave early, as I fancy James and Elizabeth both kept thoroughly short of sleep by infant Katherine. Cannot, however, deter James from driving me back to Hotel. Am greatly impressed with this chivalrous, and universal, American custom.

James and I part at the door, strawberry-clad negro porters spring to attention as I enter, and I perceive, to my horror, that General Clarence Dove is sitting in the hall, doing nothing whatever, directly between me and elevator. Turn at once to the newspaper-stand and earnestly inspect motion-picture magazines—in which I am not in the least interested—

cigars, cigarettes, and picture-postcards. Take a long time choosing six of these, and paying for them. Cannot, however, stand there all night, and am at last compelled to turn round. General Clarence Dove still immovable. Decide to bow as I go past, but without slackening speed, and this proves successful, and I go up to bed without hearing more of my book about America.

November 23rd.—Am introduced by James to important Head of Department, Miss Bassell, who kindly takes me to the White House, where I am shown State Rooms and other items of interest.

Portraits of Presidents' Wives in long rows present rather discouraging spectacle. Prefer not to dwell on these, but concentrate instead on trying to remember Who was Dolly Madison? Decide—tentatively—that she must have been an American equivalent of Nell Gwynn, but am not sufficiently sure about it to say anything to Miss B. In any case, have no idea which, if any, of America's Presidents would best bear comparison with King Charles II.

Lunch-party brings my stay in Washington

to a close, and James and Elizabeth—kind-hearted and charming to the last—take me and my luggage to the station. Am relieved to find that both look rested, and are able to assure me that dear little Katherine allowed them several hours of uninterrupted sleep.

Say good-bye to them with regret, and promise that I will come and stay with them in their first Consulate, but add proviso—perhaps rather ungraciously?—that it must be in a warm climate.

Find myself wondering as train moves out, what dear Robert will say to the number of future invitations that I have both given and accepted?

November 25th.—Philadelphia reached yesterday, and discover in myself slight and irrational tendency to repeat under my breath: "I'm off to Philadelphia in the morning." Do not know, or care, where this quotation comes from.

Unknown hostess called Mrs. Elliot receives me, and I join enormous house-party consisting of all her relations. Do not succeed, from one end of visit to the other, in discovering the name of any single one of them.

Mrs. E. says she likes *The Wide Wide World*. Am pleased at this, and we talk about it at immense length, and I tell her that a Life of Susan Warner exists, which she seems to think impossible, as she has never heard of it. Promise to send her a copy from England, and am more convinced than ever—if possible—that we are none of us prophets in our own country.

(*Mem:* Make note of Mrs. Elliot's address. Also send postcard to favorite second-hand bookseller to obtain copy of *Susan Warner* for me. Shall look extremely foolish if it isn't forthcoming, after all I've said. But must not meet trouble half-way.)

Lecture—given, unfortunately, by myself—takes place in the evening at large Club. Everyone very kind, and many intelligent questions asked, which I do my best to answer. Secretary forgets to give me my fee, and lack courage to ask for it, but it subsequently arrives by special delivery, just as I am going to bed.

November 27th.—Unexpected arrival of

guardian angel Ramona Herdman from New York. Am delighted to see her, and still more so when she gives me collection of letters from England. As usual, am on my way to book-store where I have to make short speech, and am unable to read letters in any but the most cursory way,—but ascertain that no calamity has befallen anybody, that Robert will be glad to hear when he is to meet me at Southampton, and that Caroline Concannon has written a book, and it has instantly been accepted by highly-superior publishing house. Am not in the least surprised, at this last piece of information. C.C. exactly the kind of young person to romp straight to success. Shall probably yet see small blue oval announcement on the walls of 57 Doughty Street, to the effect that they once sheltered the celebrated writer, Caroline Con-cannon. Feel that the least I can do is to cable my congratulations, and this I do, at some expense.

Miss Ramona Herdman and I then proceed to bookstore, where we meet head of depart-ment, Mrs. Kooker. Talk about Vera Brittain —*Testament of Youth* selling superbly, says

Mrs. K.—also new film, "Little Women," which everyone says I *must* see in New York— (had always meant to, anyway)—and recent adoption by American women of tomato-juice as a substitute for cocktails.

Conversation then returns to literature, and Mrs. Kooker tells me that Christmas sales will soon be coming on, but that Thanksgiving interferes with them rather badly. Try and look as if I thoroughly understood and sympathised with this, but have to give it up when she naïvely enquires whether Thanksgiving has similar disastrous effect on trade in England? Explain, as delicately as I can, that England has never, so far as I know, returned any particular thanks for occasion thus commemorated in the United States, and after a moment Mrs. K. sees this, and is amused.

Customary talk takes place—shall soon be able to say it in my sleep—and various listeners come up and speak to me kindly afterwards. Completely unknown lady in brown tells me that we met years ago, and she remembers me so well, and is so glad to see me again. Respond to this as best I can, and say—

with only too much truth—that the exact
whereabouts of our last encounter has, temporarily, escaped me. What! cries the lady re-
proachfully, have I forgotten dear old Scarborough?

As I have never in my life set foot in dear
old Scarborough, this proves very, very difficult to answer. Do not, in fact, attempt to do
so, but merely shake hands with her again and
turn attention to someone who is telling me
that she has a dear little grand-daughter, aged
five, who says most amusing things. If only,
grandmother adds wistfully, she could *remember* them, she would tell them to me, and then
I should be able to put them into a book.

Express regrets—unfortunately civil, rather
than sincere—at having to forego this privilege,
and we separate. Miss Herdman—has mysteriously produced a friend and a motor-car—tells
me that I am going with her to tea at the house
of a distinguished critic. Alexander Woollcott?
I say hopefully, and she looks rather shocked
and replies No, no, don't I remember that
A. W. lives in unique apartment in New York,
overlooking the East River? There are, she

[194]

adds curtly, other distinguished critics besides Alexander Woollcott, in America. Have not the courage, after this *gaffe*, to enquire further as to my present destination.

Tea-party, however, turns out pleasantly— which is, I feel, more than I deserve—and I enjoy myself, except when kind elderly lady— mother of hostess—suddenly exclaims that We mustn't forget we have an English woman as our guest, and immediately flings open two windows. Ice-cold wind blows in, and several people look at me—as well they may—with dislike and resentment.

Should like to tell them that nobody is more resentful of this hygienic outburst than I am myself—but cannot, of course, do so. Remind myself instead that a number of English people have been known to visit the States, only to die there of pneumonia.

Am subsequently driven back to Mrs. Elliot's by R. Herdman and friend, Miss H. informing me on the way that a speaking-engagement has been made for me at the Colony Club in New York. At this the friend suddenly interposes, and observes morosely that the Colony

Club is easily the most difficult audience in the world. They look at their wrist-watches all the time.

Can quite see what fun this must be for the speaker, and tell Miss H. that I do not think I can possibly go to the Colony Club at all—but she takes no notice.

November 28th.—New York. Return to New York, in company with Miss Herdman, and arrive at Essex House once more. Feel that this is the first step towards home, and am quite touched and delighted when clerk at bureau greets me as an old *habituée.* Feel, however, that he is disappointed in me when I am obliged to admit, in reply to enquiry, that I did *not* get to Hollywood—and was not, in fact, invited to go there. Try to make up for this by saying that I visited World's Fair at Chicago extensively—but can see that this is not at all the same thing.

Letters await me, and include one from Mademoiselle, written as usual in purple ink on thin paper, but crossed on top of front page in green—association here with Lowell Thomas —who says that she is all impatience to see me once more, it seems an affair of centuries since we met in *"ce brouhaha de New Yorck,"* and she kisses my hand with respectful affection.

(The French given to hyperbolical statements. No such performance has ever been given by Mademoiselle, or been permitted by myself to take place. Am inclined to wonder whether dear Vicky's occasional lapses from veracity may not be attributed to early influence of devoted, but not flawless, Mademoiselle?)

Just as I come to this conclusion, discover that Mademoiselle has most touchingly sent me six American Beauty roses, and immediately reverse decision as to her effect on Vicky's morals. This possibly illogical, but definitely understandable from feminine point of view.

Ring up Mademoiselle—who screeches a good deal and is difficult to hear, except for *Mon Dieu!* which occurs often—thank her for letter and roses, and ask if she can come and see a film with me to-morrow afternoon. Anything she likes, but *not* "Henry VIII." *Mais non, mais non,* Mademoiselle shrieks, and adds

[197]

something that sounds like *"ce maudit roi,"* which I am afraid refers to the Reformation, but do not enter on controversial discussion and merely suggest "Little Women" instead.

Ah, cries Mademoiselle, *voilà une bonne idée! Cette chère vie de famille—ce gentil roman de la jeunesse—cette drôle de Jo—cœur d'or—tête de linotte*—and much else that I do not attempt to disentangle.

Agree to everything, suggest lunch first— but this, Mademoiselle replies, duty will not permit—appoint meeting-place and ring off.

Immediate and urgent pre-occupation, as usual, is my hair, and retire at once to hotel beauty-parlor, where I am received with gratifying assurances that I have been missed, and competently dealt with.

Just as I get upstairs again telephone bell rings once more, and publishers demand—I think unreasonably—immediate decision as to which boat I mean to sail in, and when. Keep my head as far as possible, turn up various papers on which I feel sure I have noted steamship sailings—(but which all turn out to be memos about buying presents for the maids at

home, pictures of America for the Women's Institute, and evening stockings for myself)—
and finally plump for the *Berengaria*.

Publishers, with common-sense rather than
tenderness, at once reply that they suppose I
had better go tourist-class, as purposes of publicity have now been achieved, and it will be
much cheaper.

Assent to this, ring off, and excitedly compose cable to Robert.

November 29th.—Gratifying recrudescence of
more or less all the people met on first arrival
in New York, who ring up and ask me to lunch
or dine before I sail.

Ella Wheelwright sends round note by hand,
lavishly invites me to lunch once, and dine
twice, and further adds that she is coming to
see me off when I sail. Am touched and impressed, and accept lunch, and one dinner, and
break it to her that she will have to see me
off—if at all—tourist section. Morning filled
by visit to publishers' office, where I am kindly
received, and told that I have Laid Some Very
Useful Foundations, which makes me feel like

[199]

a Distinguished Personage at the opening of a new Town Hall.

Lecture-agent, whom I also visit, is likewise kind, but perhaps less enthusiastic, and hints that it might be an advantage if I had more than two lectures in my repertoire. Am bound to admit that this seems reasonable. He further outlines, in a light-hearted way, scheme by which I am to undertake lengthy lecture-tour next winter, extending—as far as I can make out—from New York to the furthermost point in the Rockies, and including a good deal of travelling by air.

Return modified assent to all of it, graciously accept cheque due to me, and depart.

Lunch all by myself in a Child's, and find it restful, after immense quantities of conversation indulged in of late. Service almost incredibly prompt and efficient, and find myself wondering how Americans can endure more leisurely methods so invariably prevalent in almost every country in Europe.

Soon afterwards meet Mademoiselle, and am touched—but embarrassed—by her excessive demonstrations of welcome. Have brought her small present from Chicago World's Fair, but decide not to bestow it until moment immediately preceding separation, as cannot feel at all sure what form her gratitude might take.

We enter picture-house, where I have already reserved seats—Mademoiselle exclaims a good deal over this, and says that everything in America is *un prix fou*—and Mademoiselle takes off her hat, which is large, and balances it on her knee. Ask her if this is all right, or if she hadn't better put it under the seat, and she first nods her head and then shakes it, but leaves hat where it is.

Comic film precedes "Little Women" and is concerned with the misadventures of a house-painter. Am irresistibly reminded of comic song of my youth: "When Father papered the parlor, You couldn't see Pa for paste." Am unfortunately inspired to ask Mademoiselle if she remembers it too. *Comment?* says Mademoiselle a good many times.

Explain that it doesn't matter, I will tell her about it later, it is of no importance. Mademoiselle, however, declines to be put off and I make insane excursion into French:

[201]

"*Quand mon père*"—and am then defeated. *Mais oui,* says Mademoiselle, *quand votre père* —? Cannot think how to say—"papered the parlor" in French, and make various efforts which are not a success.

We compromise at last on Mademoiselle's suggestion that *mon père* was perhaps *avec le journal dans le parloir*? which I know is incorrect, but have not the energy to improve upon.

Comic film, by this time, is fortunately over, and we prepare for "Little Women."

Well-remembered house at Concord is thrown on the screen, snow falling on the ground, and I dissolve, without the slightest hesitation, into floods of tears. Film continues unutterably moving throughout, and is beautifully acted and produced. Mademoiselle weeps beside me—can hear most people round us doing the same—and we spend entirely blissful afternoon.

Performances of Beth, Mrs. March, and Professor Bhaer seem to me artistically flawless, and Mademoiselle, between sobs, agrees with me, but immediately adds that Amy and Jo were equally good, if not better.

Repair emotional disorder as best we can, and go and drink strong coffee in nearby drug-store, when Mademoiselle's hat is discovered to be in sad state of disrepair, and she says Yes, it fell off her knee unperceived, and she thinks several people must have walked upon it. I suggest, diffidently, that we should go together and get a new one, but she says No, no, all can be put right by herself in an hour's work, and she has a small piece of black velvet and two or three artificial *blowets* from her hat of the summer before last with which to construct what will practically amount to a new hat.

The French, undoubtedly, superior to almost every other nationality in the world in thrift, ingenuity, and ability with a needle.

Talk about the children—Vicky, says Mademoiselle emotionally, remains superior to any other child she has ever met, or can ever hope to meet, for intelligence, heart and beauty. (Can remember many occasions when Mademoiselle's estimate of Vicky was far indeed from being equally complimentary.) Mademoiselle also tells me about her present pupils, with moderate enthusiasm, and speaks well of her employers—principally on the grounds that they never interfere with her, pay her an enormous salary, and are taking her back to Paris next year.

She enquires about my lecture-tour, listens sympathetically to all that I have to say, and we finally part affectionately, with an assurance from Mademoiselle that she will come and see me off on S.S. *Berengaria même*, she adds, "*si ça doit me couter la vie.*"

Feel confident that no such sacrifice will, however, be required, but slight misgiving crosses my mind, as I walk back towards Central Park, as to the reactions of Mademoiselle and Ella Wheelwright to one another, should they both carry out proposed amiable design of seeing me off.

Cheque received from lecture-bureau, and recollection of dinner engagement at Ella's apartment, encourage me to look in at shop-windows and consider the question of new evening dress, of which I am badly in need, owing to deplorable effects of repeated and unskilful packings and unpackings. Crawl along Fifth Avenue, where shops all look ex-

Go and drink strong coffee in nearby drug-store

pensive and intimidating, but definitely allur-
ing.

Venture into one of them, and am considerably dashed by the assistant, who can produce nothing but bottle-green or plum-color—
which are, she informs me, the only shades that
will be worn *at all* this year. As I look perfectly frightful in either, can see nothing for
it but to walk out again.

And then suddenly accosted in the street by
young and pretty woman with very slim legs
and large fur-collar to her coat. She says How
delightful it is to meet again, and I at once
agree, and try in vain to remember whether I
knew her in Cleveland, Chicago, Buffalo or
Boston. No success, but am moved to ask her
advice as to purchase of frocks.

Oh, she replies amiably, I must come *at once*
to her place—she is, as it happens, on her way
there now.

We proceed to her place, which turns out a
great success. No prevalence of either bottle-
green or plum-color is noticeable, and I try
on and purchase black evening frock with frills
and silver girdle. Unknown friend is charming,

buys an evening wrap and two scarves on her own account, and declares her intention of coming to see me off on the *Berengaria*.

We then part cordially, and I go back to Essex House, still—and probably for ever—unaware of her identity. Find five telephone messages waiting for me, and am rather discouraged—probably owing to fatigue—but ring up all of them conscientiously, and find that senders are mostly out. Rush of American life undoubtedly exemplified here. Am full of admiration for so much energy and vitality, but cannot possibly attempt to emulate it, and in fact go quietly to sleep for an hour before dressing for Ella's dinner-party.

This takes place in superb apartment on Park Avenue. Ella is in bottle-green—(Fifth Avenue saleswoman evidently quite right)—neck very high in front, but back and shoulders uncovered. She says that she is dying to hear about my trip. She knows that I just loved Boston, and thought myself back in England all the time I was there. She also knows that I didn't much care about Chicago, and found it very Middle-West. Just as I am preparing to contradict her, she begins to tell us all about a trip of her own to Arizona, and I get no opportunity of rectifying her entirely mistaken convictions about me and America.

Sit next man who is good-looking—though bald—and he tells me very nicely that he hears I am a great friend of Miss Blatt's. As I know only too well that he must have received this information from Miss Blatt and none other, do not like to say that he has been misinformed. We accordingly talk about Miss Blatt with earnestness and cordiality for some little while. (Sheer waste of time, no less.)

Leave early, as packing looms ahead of me and have still immense arrears of sleep to make up. Good-looking man—name is Julius van Adams—offers to drive me back, he has his own car waiting at the door. He does so, and we become absorbed in conversation—Miss Blatt now definitely forgotten—and drive five times round Central Park.

Part cordially outside Essex House in the small hours of the morning.

November 30th.—Final stages of American visit fly past with inconceivable rapidity. Con-

signment of books for the voyage is sent me,
very, very kindly, by publishers, and proves
perfectly impossible to pack, and I decide to
carry them. Everyone whom I consult says Yes,
they'll be all right in a strap. Make many reso-
lutions about purchasing a strap.

Packing, even apart from books, presents
many difficulties, and I spend much time on
all fours in hotel bedroom, amongst my belongings. Results not very satisfactory.

In the midst of it all am startled—but gratified—by sudden telephone enquiry from publishers: Have I seen anything of the Night-Life
of New York? Alternative replies to this question flash rapidly through my mind. If the
Night-Life of New York consists in returning
at late hours by taxi, through crowded streets,
from prolonged dinner-parties, then Yes. If
something more specific, then No. Have not
yet decided which line to adopt when all is
taken out of my hands. Publishers' representative, speaking through the telephone, says with
great decision that I cannot possibly be said to
have seen New York unless I have visited a
night-club and been to Harlem. He has, in

fact, arranged that I should do both. When, I ask weakly. He says, To-night, and adds—belatedly and without much sense—If that suits me. As I know, and he knows, that my engagements are entirely in the hands of himself and his firm, I accept this as a mere gesture of courtesy, and simply enquire what kind of clothes I am to wear.

(*Note:* Shampoo-and-set before to-night, and make every effort to get in a facial as well—if time permits, which it almost certainly won't.)

Later: I become part of the Night-Life of New York, and am left more or less stunned by the experience, which begins at seven o'clock when Miss Ramona Herdman comes to fetch me. She is accompanied by second charming young woman—Helen Something?—and three men, all tall. (Should like to congratulate her on this achievement but do not, of course, do so.)

Doubt crosses my mind as to whether I shall ever find anything to talk about to five complete strangers, but decide that I shall only impair my *morale* if I begin to think about that

[209]

now, and fortunately they suggest cocktails;
and these have their customary effect. (Make
mental note to the effect that the influence of
cocktails on modern life cannot be exaggerated.)
Am unable to remember the names of any of
the men but quite feel that I know them well,
and am gratified when one of them—possessor
of phenomenal eye-lashes—tells me that we
have met before. Name turns out to be Eugene,
and I gradually identify his two friends as
Charlie and Taylor, but uncertainty prevails
throughout as to which is Charlie and which is
Taylor.

Consultation takes place—in which I take
no active part—as to where we are to dine,
Miss Herdman evidently feeling responsible as
to impressions that I may derive of New York's
Night-Life. Decision finally reached that we
shall patronise a *Speak-easy de luxe*. Am much
impressed by this extraordinary contradiction
in terms.

Speak-easy is only two blocks away, we walk
there, and I am escorted by Taylor—who may
be Charlie but I think not—and he astounds
me by enquiring if from my Hotel I can hear

the lions roaring in Central Park? No, I can't. I can hear cars going by, and horns blowing, and even whistles—but no lions. Taylor evidently disappointed but suggests, as an alternative, that perhaps I have at least, in the very early mornings, heard the ducks quacking in Central Park? Am obliged to repudiate the ducks also, and can see that Taylor thinks the worse of me. He asserts, rather severely, that he himself has frequently heard both lions and ducks—I make mental resolution to avoid walking through Central Park until I know more about the whereabouts and habits of the lions —and we temporarily cease to converse.

Speak-easy de luxe turns out to be everything that its name implies—all scarlet upholstery, chromium-plating, and terrible noise —and we are privileged to meet, and talk with, the proprietor. He says he comes from Tipperary—(I have to stifle immediate impulse to say that It's a long, long way to Tipperary)— and we talk about Ireland, London night-clubs, and the Empire State Building. Charlie is suddenly inspired to say—without foundation— that I want to know what will happen to the speak-easy when Prohibition is repealed? To this the proprietor replies—probably with perfect truth—that he is, he supposes, asked that question something like one million times every evening—and shortly afterwards he leaves us.

Dinner is excellent, we dance at intervals, and Eugene talks to me about books and says he is a publisher.

We then depart in a taxi, for night-club, and I admire—not for the first time—the amount of accommodation available in American taxis. We all talk, and discuss English food, of which Ramona and her friend Helen speak more kindly than it deserves—probably out of consideration for my feelings. Eugene and Charlie preserve silence—no doubt for the same reason —but Taylor, evidently a strong-minded person, says that he has suffered a good deal from English cabbage. Savories, on the other hand, are excellent. They are eaten, he surprisingly adds, with a special little knife and fork, usually of gold. Can only suppose that Taylor, when in England, moves exclusively in ducal circles, and hastily resolve never in any circumstances to ask him to my own house where savories, if any, are eaten off perfectly ordinary electro-plate.

Night-club is reached—name over the door in electric light is simply—but inappropriately —*Paradise*. It is, or seems to me, about the size of the Albert Hall, and is completely packed with people all screaming at the tops of their voices, orchestra playing jazz, and extremely pretty girls with practically no clothes on at all, prancing on a large stage.

We sit down at a table, and Charlie immediately tells me that the conductor of the band is Paul Whiteman, and that he lost 75 lbs. last year and his wife wrote a book. I scream back Really? and decide that conversationally I can do no more, as surrounding noise is too overwhelming.

Various young women come on and perform unnatural contortions with their bodies, and I indulge in reflections on the march of civilisation, but am roused from this by Taylor, who roars into my ear that the conductor of the orchestra is Whiteman, and he has recently lost 75 lbs. in weight. Content myself this time with nodding in reply.

[213]

Noise continues deafening, and am moved by the sight of three exhausted-looking women in black velvet, huddled round a microphone on platform and presumably singing into it—but no sound audible above surrounding din. They are soon afterwards eclipsed by further instalment of entirely undressed *houris*, each waving wholly inadequate feather-fan.

Just as I am deciding that no one over the age of twenty-five should be expected to derive satisfaction from watching this display, Taylor again becomes my informant. The proprietors of this place, he bellows, are giving the self-same show, absolutely free, to four hundred little newsboys on Thanksgiving Day. Nothing, I reply sardonically, could possibly be healthier or more beneficial to the young—but this sarcasm entirely wasted as it is inaudible, and shortly afterwards we leave. Air of Broadway feels like purity itself, after the atmosphere prevalent inside *Paradise*, which might far more suitably be labelled exactly the opposite.

Now, I enquire, are we going to Harlem? Everyone says Oh no, it's no use going to Har-

lem before one o'clock in the morning at the
very earliest. We are going to another night-
club on Broadway. This one is called *Mont-
martre*, and is comparatively small and quiet.

This actually proves to be the case, and am
almost prepared to wager that not more than
three hundred people are sitting round the
dance-floor screaming at one another. Orchestra
is very good indeed—colored female pianist
superlatively so—and two young gentlemen, ac-
claimed as "The Twins" and looking about fifteen years of age, are dancing admirably. We
watch this for some time, and reward it with
well-deserved applause. Conversation is comparatively audible, and on the whole I can hear
quite a number of the things we are supposed
to be talking about. These comprise Mae West,
the World's Fair in Chicago, film called "The
Three Little Pigs," and the difference in pro-
grammes between the American Radio and the
British Broadcasting Corporation.

Charlie tells me that he has not read my
book—which doesn't surprise me—and adds
that he will certainly do so at once—which we

both know to be a polite gesture and not to be taken seriously.

Conviction gradually invades me that I am growing sleepy and that in another minute I shan't be able to help yawning. Pinch myself under the table and look round at Helen and Ramona, but both seem to be perfectly fresh and alert. Involuntary and most unwelcome reflection crosses my mind that *age will tell*. Yawn becomes very imminent indeed and I set my teeth, pinch harder than ever, and open my eyes as widely as possible. Should be sorry indeed to see what I look like, at this juncture, but am fortunately spared the sight. Taylor is now talking to me—I think about a near relation of his own married to a near relation of an English Duke—but all reaches me through a haze, and I dimly hear myself saying automatically at short intervals that I quite agree with him, and he is perfectly right.

Situation saved by orchestra, which breaks into the "Blue Danube," and Eugene, who invites me to dance. This I gladly do and am restored once more to wakefulness. This is still further intensified by cup of black coffee which

I drink immediately after sitting down again, and yawn is temporarily defeated.

Eugene talks about publishing, and I listen with interest, except for tendency to look at his enormous eye-lashes and wonder if he has any sisters, and if theirs are equally good.

Presently Ramona announces that it is two o'clock, and what about Harlem? We all agree that Harlem is the next step, and once more emerge into the night.

By the time we are all in a taxi, general feeling has established itself that we are all old friends, and know one another very well indeed. I look out at the streets, marvellously lighted, and remember that I must get Christmas presents for the maids at home. Decide on two pairs of silk stockings for Florence, who is young, but Cook presents more difficult problem. Cannot believe that silk stockings would be really acceptable, and in any case feel doubtful of obtaining requisite size. What about hand-bag? Not very original, and could be equally well obtained in England. Book out of the question, as Cook has often remarked, in my hearing, that reading is a sad waste of time.

At this juncture Taylor suddenly remarks that he sees I am extremely observant, I take mental notes of my surroundings all the time, and he has little doubt that I am, at this very moment, contrasting the night-life of America with the night-life to which I am accustomed in London and Paris. I say Yes, Yes, and try not to remember that the night-life to which I am accustomed begins with letting out the cat at half-past ten and winding the cuckoo-clock, and ends with going straight to bed and to sleep until eight o'clock next morning.

Slight pause follows Taylor's remark, and I try to look as observant and intelligent as I can, but am relieved when taxi stops, and we get out at the Cotton Club, Harlem.

Colored girls, all extremely nude, are dancing remarkably well on stage, colored orchestra is playing—we all say that, of course, they understand Rhythm as nobody else in the world does—and the usual necessity prevails of screaming very loudly in order to be heard above all the other people who are screaming very loudly.

(*Query:* Is the effect of this perpetual

[218]

Colored girls . . . dancing remarkably well

shrieking repaid by the value of the remarks we exchange? *Answer:* Definitely, No.)

Colored dancers, after final terrific jerkings, retire, and spectators rise up from their tables and dance to the tune of "Stormy Weather," and we all say things about Rhythm all over again.

Sleep shortly afterwards threatens once more to overwhelm me, and I drink more black coffee. At half-past three Ramona suggests that perhaps we have now explored the night-life of New York sufficiently, I agree that we have, and the party breaks up. I say that I have enjoyed my evening—which is perfectly true—and thank them all very much.

Take one look at myself in the glass on reaching my room again, and decide that gay life is far from becoming to me, at any rate at four o'clock in the morning.

Last thought before dropping to sleep is that any roaring that may be indulged in by the lions of Central Park under my window will probably pass unnoticed by me, after hearing the orgy of noise apparently inseparable from the night-life of New York.

December 1st.—Attend final lunch-party, given by Ella Wheelwright, and at which she tells me that I shall meet Mr. Allen. Experience strong inclination to scream and say that I can't, I'm the only person in America who hasn't read his book—but Ella says No, no—she doesn't mean Hervey Allen at all, she means Frederick Lewis Allen, who did *American Procession.* This, naturally, is a very different thing, and I meet Mr. Allen and his wife with perfect calm, and like them both very much. Also meet English Colonel Roddie, author of *Peace Patrol,* which I haven't read, but undertake to buy for Robert's Christmas present, as I think it sounds as though he might like it.

Female guests consist of two princesses—one young and the other elderly, both American, and both wearing enormous pearls. Am reminded of Lady B. and experience uncharitable wish that she could be here, as pearls far larger than hers, and reinforced with colossal diamonds and sapphires into the bargain. Wish also that convention and good manners alike did not forbid my frankly asking the nearest princess to let me have a good look at her black

[220]

pearl ring, diamond bracelet, and wrist-watch set in rubies and emeralds.

Remaining lady strikes happy medium be-tween dazzling display of princesses, and my own total absence of anything except old-fashioned gold wedding-ring—not even plati-num—and modest diamond ring inherited from Aunt Julia and tells me that she is the wife of a stock broker. I ought, she thinks, to see the New York Exchange, and it will be a pleasure to take me all over it. Thank her very much, and explain that I am sailing at four o'clock to-morrow. She says: We could go in the morning. Again thank her very much, but my packing is not finished, and am afraid it will be impossi-ble. Then, she says indomitably, what about this afternoon? It could, she is sure, be man-aged. Thank her more than ever, and again decline, this time without giving any specific reason for doing so.

She is unresentful, and continues to talk to me very nicely after we have left the dining-room. Ella and the two princesses ignore us both, and talk to one another about Paris, the Riviera, and clothes.

[221]

Ella, however, just before I take my leave, undergoes a slight change of heart—presumably —and reminds me that she has promised to come and see me off, and will lunch with me at the Essex and take me to the docks. She unexpectedly adds that she is sending me round a book for the voyage—*Anthony Adverse.* Am horrified, but not in the least surprised, to hear myself thanking her effusively, and saying how very much I shall look forward to reading it.

Stock-broking lady offers me a lift in her car, and we depart together. She again makes earnest endeavor on behalf of the Stock Exchange, but I am unable to meet her in any way, though grateful for evidently kind intention.

Fulfill absolutely final engagement, which is at Colony Club, where I naturally remember recent information received, that the members do nothing but look at their wrist-watches. This, fortunately for me, turns out to be libellous, at least so far as present audience is concerned. All behave with the utmost decorum, and I deliver lecture, and conclude by reading short extract from my own published work.

Solitary *contretemps* of the afternoon occurs here, when I hear lady in front row enquire of her neighbor: What is she going to read? Neighbor replies in lugubrious accents that she doesn't know, but it will be *funny*. Feel that after this no wit of mine, however brilliant, could be expected to succeed.

Day concludes with publisher calling for me in order to take me to a party held at Englewood, New Jersey. He drives his own car, with the result that we lose the way and arrive very late. Host says, Didn't we get the little map that he sent out with the invitation? Yes, my publisher says, he got it all right, but unfortunately left it at home. Feel that this is exactly the kind of thing I might have done myself.

Pleasant evening follows, but am by now far too much excited by the thought of sailing for home to-morrow to give my mind to anything else.

December 2nd.—Send purely gratuitous cable to Robert at dawn saying that I am Just Off— which I shan't be till four o'clock this afternoon—and then address myself once more to packing, with which I am still struggling when Ella Wheelwright is announced. She is, she says, too early, but she thought she might be able to help me.

This she does by sitting on bed and explaining to me that dark-red varnish doesn't really suit her nails. Coral, yes, rose-pink, yes. But not dark-red. Then why, I naturally enquire—with my head more or less in a suit-case—does she put it on? Why? Ella repeats in astonishment. Because she has to, of course. It's the only color that anyone is wearing now, so naturally, she has no alternative. But it's too bad, because the color really doesn't suit her at all, and in fact she dislikes it.

I make sounds that I hope may pass as sympathetic—though cannot really feel that Ella has made out a very good case for herself as a victim of unkind Fate—and go on packing and —still more—unpacking.

Impossibility of fitting in present for Our Vicar's Wife, besides dressing-slippers and travelling-clock of my own, overcomes me altogether, and I call on Ella for help. This she reluctantly gives, but tells me at the same time that her dress wasn't meant for a strain of any kind, and may very likely split under the arms if she tries to lift anything.

This catastrophe is fortunately spared us, and boxes are at last closed and taken downstairs, hand-luggage remaining in mountainous-looking pile, surmounted by tower of books. Ella looks at these with distaste, and says that what I need is a Strap, and then immediately presents me with *Anthony Adverse*. Should feel much more grateful if she had only brought me a strap instead.

We go down to lunch in Persian Coffee Shop, and talk about Mrs. Tressider, to whom Ella sends rather vague messages, of which only one seems to me at all coherent—to the effect that she hopes The Boy is stronger than he was. I promise to deliver it, and even go so far as to suggest that I should write and let Ella know what I think of The Boy next time I see him. She very sensibly replies that I really needn't trouble to do that, and I dismiss entire scheme forthwith. Discover after lunch that rain is pouring down in torrents, and facetiously remark that I may as well get used to it again, as I shall probably find the same state of affairs on reaching England. Ella makes chilly reply to the effect that the British climate always seems to her to be thoroughly maligned, especially by the English—which makes me feel that I have been unpatriotic. She then adds that she only hopes this doesn't mean that the *Berengaria* is in for a rough crossing.

Go upstairs to collect my belongings in mood of the deepest dejection. Books still as unmanageable as ever, and I eventually take nine of them, and Ella two, and carry them downstairs.

Achieve the docks by car, Ella driving. She again reiterates that I ought to have got a strap —especially when we find that long walk awaits us before we actually reach gangway of the *Berengaria*.

Hand-luggage proves too much for me altogether, and I twice drop various small articles, and complete avalanche of literature. Ella— who is comparatively lightly laden—walks on well ahead of me and has sufficient presence of mind not to look behind her—which is on the whole a relief to me.

Hand-luggage proves too much for me

Berengaria looks colossal, and thronged with people. Steward, who has been viewing my progress with—or without—the books, compassionately, detaches himself from the crowd and comes to my assistance. He will, he says, take me—and books—to my cabin.

Ella and I then follow him for miles and miles, and Ella says thoughtfully that I should be a long way from the deck, if there was a fire.

Cabin is filled, in the most gratifying way, with flowers and telegrams. Also several parcels which undoubtedly contain more books. Steward leaves us, and Ella sits on the edge of the bunk and says that when she took her last trip to Europe her stateroom was exactly like a florist's shop. Even the stewardess said she'd never seen anything like it, in fifteen years' experience.

Then, I reply with spirit, she couldn't ever have seen a film-star travelling. Film-stars, to my certain knowledge, have to engage one, if not two, extra cabins solely to accommodate flowers, fruit, literature and other gifts bestowed upon them. This remark not a success

[227]

with Ella—never thought it would be—and she says very soon afterwards that perhaps I should like to unpack and get straight, and she had better leave me.

Escort her on deck—lose the way several times and thoughts again revert to probable unpleasant situation in the event of a fire—and we part.

Ella's last word to me is an assurance that she will be longing to hear of my safe arrival, and everyone always laughs at her because she gets such quantities of night-letters and cables from abroad, but how can she help it, if she has so many friends? Mine to her is—naturally—an expression of gratitude for all her kindness. We exchange final reference to Mrs. Tressider, responsible for bringing us together—she is to be given Ella's love—The Boy should be outgrowing early delicacy by this time—and I lean over the side and watch Ella, elegant to the last in hitherto unknown grey squirrel coat, take her departure.

Look at fellow-travellers surrounding me, and wonder if I am going to like any of them —outlook not optimistic, and doubtless they

feel the same about me. Suddenly perceive
familiar figure—Mademoiselle is making her
way towards me. She mutters *Dieu! quelle
canaille!*—which I think is an unnecessarily
strong way of expressing herself—and I remove
myself and her to adjacent saloon, where we sit
in armchairs and Mademoiselle presents me
with a small chrysanthemum in a pot.

She is in very depressed frame of mind, sheds
tears, and tells me that many a fine ship has
been *onglouti par les vagues* and that it breaks
her heart to think of my two unhappy little
children left without their mother. I beg
Mademoiselle to take a more hopeful outlook,
but at this she shows symptoms of being of-
fended, so hastily add that I have often known
similar misgivings myself—which is true. *Ah,*
replies Mademoiselle lugubriously, *les pressentiments, les pressentiments!* and we are again
plunged in gloom.

Suggest taking her to see my cabin, as afford-
ing possible distraction, and we accordingly
proceed there, though not by any means without
difficulty.

Mademoiselle, at sight of telegrams, again

says *Mon Dieu!* and begs me to open them at once, in case of bad news. I do so, and am able to assure her that they contain only amiable wishes for a good journey from kind American friends. Mademoiselle—evidently in over-wrought condition altogether—does not receive this as I had hoped, but breaks into floods of tears and says that she is suffering from *mal du pays* and *la nostalgie.*

Mistake this for neuralgia, and suggest aspirin, and this error fortunately restores Mademoiselle to comparative cheerfulness. Does not weep again until we exchange final and affectionate farewells on deck, just as gang-plank is about to be removed. *Vite!* shrieks Mademoiselle, dashing down it, and achieving the dock in great disarray.

I wave good-bye to her, and *Berengaria* moves off. Dramatic moment of bidding Fare-well to America is then entirely ruined for me by unknown Englishwoman who asks me severely if that was a friend of mine?

Yes, it was.

Very well. It reminds her of an extraordinary occasion when her son was seeing her off from

Southampton. He remained too long in the cabin—very devoted son, anxious to see that all was comfortable for his mother—and when he went up on deck, what do I think had happened?

Can naturally guess this without the slightest difficulty, but feel that it would spoil the story if I do, so only What? in anxious tone of voice, as though I had no idea at all. The ship, says unknown Englishwoman impressively, had moved several yards away from the dock. And what do I suppose her son did then?

He swam, I suggest.

Not at all. He jumped. Put one hand on the rail, and simply leapt. And he just made it. One inch less, and he would have been in the water. But as it was, he just landed on the dock. It was a most frightful thing to do, and upset her for the whole voyage. She couldn't get over it at all. Feel rather inclined to suggest that she hasn't really got over it yet, if she is compelled to tell the story to complete stranger— but have no wish to be unsympathetic, so reply instead that I am glad it all ended well. Yes, says Englishwoman rather resentfully—but it upset her for the rest of the voyage.

Can see no particular reason why this conversation should ever end, and less reason still why it should go on, so feel it better to smile and walk away, which I do. Stewardess comes to my cabin later, and is very nice and offers to bring vases for flowers. Some of them, she thinks, had better go on my table in dining-saloon.

I thank her and agree, and look at letters, telegrams and books. Am gratified to discover note from Mr. Alexander Woollcott, no less. He has, it appears, two very distinguished friends also travelling on the *Berengaria*, and they will undoubtedly come and introduce themselves to me, and make my acquaintance. This will, writes Mr. W. gracefully, be to the great pleasure and advantage of us all.

Am touched, but know well that none of it will happen, (a) because the distinguished friends are travelling first-class and I am not, and (b) because I shall all too certainly be laid low directly the ship gets into the open

[232]

sea, and both unwilling and unable to make acquaintance with anybody.

Unpack a few necessities—am forcibly reminded of similar activities on S. S. *Statendam* and realise afresh that I really am on my way home and need not become agitated at mere sight of children's photographs—and go in search of dining-saloon.

Find myself at a table with three Canadian young gentlemen who all look to me exactly alike certainly brothers, and quite possibly triplets—and comparatively old acquaintance whose son performed athletic feat on Southampton docks.

Enormous mountain of flowers decorates the middle of the table—everybody says Where do these come from? and I admit ownership and am evidently thought the better of thenceforward.

Much greater triumph, however, awaits me when table-steward, after taking a good look at me, suddenly proclaims that he and I were on board S.S. *Mentor* together, in 1922. Overlook possibly scandalous interpretation to which his words may lend themselves, and ad-

[233]

mit to S.S. *Mentor*. Table-steward, in those days, was with the Blue Funnel line. He had the pleasure, he says, of waiting upon my husband and myself at the Captain's table. He remembers us perfectly, and I have changed very little.

At this my *prestige* quite obviously goes up by leaps and bounds, and English fellow-traveller—name turns out to be Mrs. Smiley—and Canadian triplets all gaze at me with awe-stricken expressions.

Behavior of table-steward does nothing towards diminishing this, as he makes a point of handing everything to me first, and every now and then breaks off in the performance of his duties to embark on agreeable reminiscences of our earlier acquaintance.

Am grateful for so much attention, but feel very doubtful if I shall be able to live up to it all through voyage.

December 4th.—Flowers have to be removed from cabin, and books remain unread, but stewardess is kindness itself and begs me not to think of moving.

I do not think of moving.

December 5th.—Stewardess tells me that storm has been frightful, and surpassed any in her experience. Am faintly gratified at this—Why?—and try not to think that she probably says exactly the same thing more or less every voyage to every sea-sick passenger.

Practically all her ladies, she adds impressively, have been laid low, and one of the stewardesses. And this reminds her: the table-steward who looks after me in the dining-saloon has enquired many times how I am getting on, and if there is anything I feel able to take, later on, I have only to let him know.

Am touched by this, and decide that I could manage a baked potato and a dry biscuit. These are at once provided, and do me a great deal of good. The stewardess encourages me, says that the sea is now perfectly calm, and that I shall feel better well wrapped up on deck.

Feel that she is probably right, and follow her advice. Am quite surprised to see numbers of healthy-looking people tramping about vigorously, and others—less active, but still robust—sitting in chairs with rugs round their legs. Take up this attitude myself, but turn my

[235]

back to the Atlantic Ocean, which does not seem to me quite to deserve eulogies bestowed upon it by stewardess. Canadian triplets presently go past—all three wearing black berets—and stop and ask how I am. They have, they say, missed me in the dining-room. I enquire How they are getting on with Mrs. Smiley? and they look at one another with rather hunted expressions, and one of them says Oh, she talks a good deal.

Can well believe it.

Alarming thought occurs to me that she may be occupying the chair next mine, but inspection of card on the back of it reveals that this is not so, and that I am to be privileged to sit next to Mr. H. Cyril de Mullins Green. Am, most unjustly, at once conscious of being strongly prejudiced against him. Quote Shakespeare to myself in a very literary way— What's in a Name?—and soon afterwards doze.

Day passes with extreme slowness, but not unpleasantly. Decide that I positively must write and thank some of the people who so kindly sent me flowers and books for journey, but am quite unable to rouse myself to the extent of fetching writing materials from cabin.

Take another excursion into the realms of literature and quote to myself from Mrs. Gamp:
"Rouge yourself, Mr. Chuffy"—but all to no
avail.

Later in the afternoon Mr. H. Cyril de
Mullins Green materialises as pale young man
with horn-rimmed glasses and enormous shock
of black hair. He tells me—in rather resentful
tone of voice—that he knows my name, and
adds that he writes himself. Feel inclined to
reply that I Thought as Much—but do not do
so. Enquire instead—though not without misgivings as to tactfulness of the question—with
whom the works of Mr. H. C. de M. G. are
published? He mentions a firm of which I have
never heard, and I reply Oh really? as if I had
known all about them for years, and the conversation drops. Remain on deck for dinner,
but have quite a good one nevertheless, and
immediately afterwards go down below.

December 6th.—Receive radio from Robert,
saying All Well and he will meet me at Southampton. This has definitely bracing effect, and
complete recovery sets in.

Mrs. Smiley, in my absence, has acquired

complete domination over Canadian triplets, and monopolises conversation at meals. She appears only moderately gratified by my restoration to health, and says that she herself has kept her feet throughout. She has, also, won a great deal at Bridge, played deck tennis, and organised a treasure-hunt which was a great success. To this neither I nor the Canadians have anything to counter, but after a time the youngest-looking of the triplets mutters rather defiantly that they have walked four miles every day, going round and round the deck. I applaud this achievement warmly, and Mrs. Smiley says that Those calculations are often defective, which silences us all once more.

Learn that concert has been arranged for the evening—Mrs. Smiley has taken very active part in organising this and is to play several accompaniments—and H. Cyril de Mullins G. tells me later that he hopes it won't give great offence if he keeps away, but he cannot endure amateur performances of any sort or kind. As for music, anything other than Bach is pure torture to him. I suggest that in that case he must suffer quite a lot in the dining-saloon

[238]

He writes himself

where music quite other than Bach is played
regularly, and he asks in a pained way whether
I haven't noticed that he very seldom comes to
the dining-saloon at all? He cannot, as a rule,
endure the sight of his fellow-creatures eating.
It revolts him. For his own part, he very seldom eats anything at all. No breakfast, an apple
for lunch, and a little red wine, fish and fruit
in the evening is all that he ever requires. I say,
rather enviously, How cheap! and suggest that
this must make housekeeping easy for his
mother, but H. C. de M. G. shudders a good
deal and replies that he hasn't lived with his
parents for years and years and thinks family
life extremely *bourgeois*. As it seems obvious
that Cyril and I differ on almost every point
of importance, I decide that we might as well
drop the conversation, and open new novel by
L. A. G. Strong that I want to read.

Modern fiction! says Cyril explosively. How
utterly lousy it all is. He will, he admits, give
me Shaw—(for whom I haven't asked)—but
there are no writers living to-day. Not one. I
say Come, Come, what about ourselves? but
Mr. de M. G. evidently quite impervious to this

witty shaft and embarks on very long mono-
logue, in the course of which he demolishes
many world-wide reputations. Am extremely
thankful when we are interrupted by Mrs.
Smiley, at the sight of whom C. de M. G. at
once gets onto his feet and walks away. (De-
duce from this that they have met before.)

Mrs. Smiley has come, she tells me, in order
to find out if I will give a little Reading from
Something of my Own at to-night's concert.
No, I am very sorry, but I cannot do anything
of the kind. Now *why*? Mrs. S. argumenta-
tively enquires. No one will be critical, in fact
as likely as not they won't listen, but it will
give pleasure. Do I not believe in brightening
this sad old world when I get the chance? For
Mrs. Smiley's own part, she never grudges a
little trouble if it means happiness for others.
Naturally, getting up an entertainment of this
kind means hard work, and probably no thanks
at the end of it—but she feels it's a duty. That's
all. Just simply a duty. I remain unresponsive,
and Mrs. S. shakes her head and leaves me.

(If I see or hear any more of Mrs. S. shall
almost certainly feel it my duty, if not my

pleasure, to kick her overboard at earliest possible opportunity.)

Concert duly takes place, in large saloon, and everyone—presumably with the exception of Cyril—attends it. Various ladies sing ballads, mostly about gardens, or little boys with sticky fingers—a gentleman plays a concertina solo, not well—and another gentleman does conjuring tricks. Grand *finale* is a topical song, said to have been written by Mrs. Smiley, into which references to all her fellow-passengers are introduced, not without ingenuity. Should much like to know how she has found out so much about them all in the time.

Appeal is then made—by Mrs. Smiley—for Naval Charity to which we are all asked to subscribe—Mrs. Smiley springs round the room with a tambourine, and we all drop coins into it—and we disperse.

Obtain glimpse, as I pass smoking-saloon, of Mr. H. Cyril de Mullins Green drinking what looks like brandy-and-soda, and telling elderly gentleman—who has, I think, reached senility —that English Drama has been dead—absolutely *dead*—ever since the Reformation.

December 7th.—Pack for—I hope—the last time, and spend most of the day listening to various reports that We shan't be in before midnight, We shall get in by four o'clock this afternoon, and We can't get in to-day at all.

Finally notice appears on a board outside dining-saloon, informing us that we shall get to Southampton at 9 P.M. and that dinner will be served at six—(which seems to me utterly unreasonable)—luggage to be ready and outside cabins at four o'clock. (More unreasonable still.) Every possible preparation is completed long before three o'clock, and I feel quite unable to settle down to anything at all, and am reduced to watching Mrs. Smiley play table-tennis with one of the Canadian triplets, and beat him into a cocked hat.

Dinner takes place at six o'clock—am far too much excited to eat any—and from thence onward I roam uneasily about from one side of ship to the other, and think that every boat I see is tender from Southampton conveying Robert to meet me.

Am told at last by deck-steward—evidently

feeling sorry for me—that tender is the *other* side, and I rush there accordingly, and hang over the side and wave passionately to familiar figure in blue suit. Familiar figure turns out to be that of complete stranger.

Scan everybody else in advancing tender, and decide that I have at last sighted Robert —raincoat and felt hat— but nerve has been rather shattered and am doubtful about waving. This just as well, as raincoat is afterwards claimed by unknown lady in tweed coat and skirt, who screams: Is that you, Dad? and is in return hailed with: Hello, Mum, old girl! how are you?

I decide that Robert has (a) had a stroke from excitement (b) been summoned to the death-bed of one of the children (c) missed the tender.

Remove myself from the rail in dejection, and immediately come face to face with Robert, who has mysteriously boarded the ship unperceived. Am completely overcome, and disgrace myself by bursting into tears.

Robert pats me very kindly and strolls away

and looks at entirely strange pile of luggage whilst I recover myself. Recovery is accelerated by Mrs. Smiley who comes up and asks me If that is my husband? to which I reply curtly that it is, and turn my back on her.

Robert and I sit down on sofa outside the dining-saloon, and much talk follows, only interrupted by old friend the table-steward, who hurries out and greets Robert with great enthusiasm, and says that he will personally see my luggage through the Customs.

This he eventually does, with the result that we get through with quite unnatural rapidity, and have a choice of seats in boat-train. Say good-bye to old friend cordially, and with suitable recognition of his services.

Robert tells me that He is Glad to See Me Again, and that the place has been very quiet. I tell him in return that I never mean to leave home again as long as I live, and ask if there are any letters from the children?

There is one from each, and I am delighted. Furthermore, says Robert, Our Vicar's Wife sent her love, and hopes that we will both come to tea on Thursday, five o'clock *not* earlier, because of the Choir Practice.

Agree with the utmost enthusiasm that this will be delightful, and feel that I am indeed Home again.

THE END